2084

Julie Clark

Published by JRC Publications

ISBN: 978-1-4457-3167-4

1

"Odyssey, load NWL News, Cinematic mode", squealed Anna, who was already eagerly perched in the viewing area at the front of the room.

Her crutches rested nearby, their shafts wrapped in a pretty floral fabric; a cheerful mosaic, and deliberate attempt to divert attention from her missing left limb.

The room hummed to life, as a curtain of luminous, crystalline emerald cascaded down the smooth surface of the wall, illuminating the sterility of the hospital bay. The floating, shimmering particles assembled, to form a razor-thin, translucent screen.

Nurse Andrews dropped an armful of towels and rushed to help Holly, who was shuffling across the floor, twisted in pain, her skin a patchwork of angry scars, and a constant, cruel reminder of the past.

The three women made themselves comfortable on a white velour sofa, as the Scales of Justice, The People's Justice emblem, hovered before them; a serene beacon of peace, and a chilling warning, to anyone who dare defy the New World Law.

Jessie, another patient at the Shoreland Centre, was paralysed from the waist down and wired to a brain monitor but pushed herself up into a sitting position.

"What's going on?", she shouted, trying to be heard over the dramatic mid-day news intro.

"Shush, just listen", snapped Anna.

The floating image exploded into a galaxy of glowing pixels, as beams of light burst from the screen, darting like searchlights. As the rays united, a three-dimensional figure materialised, his ghostly form seemingly levitating in mid-air, as he began his broadcast.

"Here is the announcement that the world has been waiting for, the date for Garth Sutton's Final Justice, where you can see the killer face his fate.

Sutton, who appeared in court 2 years ago in 2082, was found guilty of the abduction of two 21-year-old women and the murder of a 22-year-old man.

The women's testimonies revealed that Sutton had used a police department vehicle and flagged them down, as they travelled home at night on a secluded country road.

They were forced at gunpoint into the van, where they had lost consciousness. They awoke bound and gagged, in what they believed was a large, underground bunker.

Here they were held captive by single, 54-year-old Sutton for almost 12 months, during which time he drugged, tortured, and sexually abused them.

The women described in detail, how the young man suffered a harrowing death at the hands of the monster.

They also claimed to have witnessed shocking evidence of the grisly remains of previous victims, and explained how Sutton would watch sadistic, homemade snuff movies before carrying out his attacks.

To reveal the full extent of Sutton's crimes, the judge granted permission to involve the controversial Organisation, The People's Justice, and the trial was adjourned.

Sutton underwent a mind-sweep, a non-invasive procedure, which extracts the subject's memories, captured in the form of images. These images are now stored within the Organisations Mind Vault, and available for the public to view.

This astounding technology has been vastly developed over the last 80 years since the discovery of brain fingerprinting; there is now no doubt of a perpetrator's guilt.

The killer's memories revealed that over a 30-year period he had taken the lives of 72 innocent people, 2 of which were children, and the shocking truth was uncovered.

The victims were identified, and their families informed, most of whom were present at what the press had named, The Final Trial.

The Jury, who had the arduous task of watching the sickening evidence over the course of 12 weeks, deliberated for less than 45 minutes, before returning with a unanimous verdict of guilty on all counts.

Sutton was reported to have dropped to his knees, his head buried in his hands, and shaking uncontrollably, as the packed courtroom erupted in deafening cheers.

Each of the Jurors requested mind cleansing, to erase all trace of the horror which they had witnessed.

We will now hear the Judge's final statement, released today".

"Garth Sutton is without a doubt, one of the most evil and depraved killers of all time. The shocking evidence is absolute and undeniable.

Sutton is detained at The People's Justice Organisation, under armed guard, whilst being prepared to receive his punishment.

I implore you, please visit the PJO's Vault to watch his disturbing memories. Learn of the man who slaughtered his victims for his own twisted, sexual gratification.

Watch the surviving victim's ordeals, and the fate of their friend, who tragically, never survived the clutches of evil.

See heart-breaking photographs of 5-year-old Rose, and the remains of his youngest, tiny victim, through Sutton's own eyes.

For many of you, I believe this will be more than enough for you to extend his sentence.

Help us, to help you live in a world of peace, and together we can work at instilling fear, to deter people from ever committing these offences.

We will not sit back and let the evil which exists within society take hold and rule.

Abide by the New World Law.

Defiance will *not* be tolerated!".

"That was the Honourable Judge Tyler, delivering a powerful, final statement regarding the Garth Sutton case.

Sutton's memories are now available for public viewing in the Justice Vault, so please, get voting!

I will now read a heart-breaking statement from the parents of Rose Foster, abducted from the family home, more than 11 years ago.

'There are no words to describe the agony which my wife and I have felt, since the murder of our beautiful daughter, Rose.

Our innocent baby girl endured days of unimaginable agony and terror, before Sutton ended her life in the most horrific of ways. He ensured that we were left in no doubt that our little girl had suffered beyond comprehension.

Rose died at the hands of one of the most despicable, evil pieces of shit to ever have walked this earth!

In honour of the victims, please give us some sort of closure. We know we will never get our loved ones back, but we deserve to see their killer suffer, for as long as possible, for so cruelly ending their lives.

We beg you, please vote for an extended sentence. Evil such as this deserves no mercy!'.

That was an emotional plea from the father of Sutton's youngest victim.

Tickets for the Final Justice Show have now sold out, so please make sure you're tuned in to the Vault on Saturday, the 26th of August at 10pm, where you can watch Sutton receive his punishment live!

Now, over to Charlotte for the weather…"

"Odyssey, off", said Nurse Andrews, and the diamond screen dissolved, leaving a green, mystical aura, which slowly faded away.

Anna and Holly struggled back to their beds.

There was total silence in the room, as the nurse collected the empty medication cups, and headed towards the door.

"Girls, try to get some rest, I'll see you all later", she said, as the bay doors closed behind her.

"What was all that about?", asked Jessie with questioning eyes, but her mind began to drift, as it often did, and Anna's replies fell on deaf ears.

2

The People's Justice Organisation
Visitor's Suite

"Are you certain you want to go through with this, it's not too late to change your minds?", Richard asked the girls.

"Yes, we must do this", Heather said, looking to Abbie, who nodded nervously in reply.

"Holography and artificial intelligence can take over and improvise at any time, should either of you wish to leave, just shout 'stop', and the AI robots will take over. As you know, I'm here at the PJO and in the V.R. program most of the time, so I'll never be far away. Please don't feel that once you're inside that there's no escape", said Richard.

"It's okay, we understand", Heather assured him, as she took Abbie's hand.

"Okay. You can see Sutton before going in. It's going to be extremely difficult for you both, but we thought it best, rather than to face him for the first time since… well, you know… to put your minds at rest there's no danger and …"

Abbie interrupted, "We must do this".

"As long as you're both sure. Follow me", he smiled.

Abbie and Heather followed Richard down a bright corridor, passing tinted windows on either side. The departments were like a honeycomb design, each hexagonal room was adjoined and accessible to the next.

The hustle of employees entering their workplaces made an almost tune-like sound, with the gentle beep of eye-scanners and doors sliding open and shut.

The corridor began to widen, as they reached a steel security door, its sheer size intimidating. The words 'Detention Vault' were deeply etched into the metal, above the door.

Richard pressed a silver button on a small intercom, set to the right on the wall, and a middle-aged man, with a bristly, fiery moustache and swarthy complexion came into view.

"Detention Vault Security, can I help you?", his powerful voice sounded.

"Hello, I'm Richard Foster, I…",

"We've been expecting you", the man interrupted.

"Position yourselves within the border of the scanner marker and remain still for identification and security checks", he ordered sternly.

"Of course, sure", nodded Richard, as he gently ushered the girls backwards.

They stood together within a large, circular border on the floor. A thick halo of electric blue began to descend, encasing them within a cocoon of dusty light, which reached the floor in seconds – a powdery puff of pale-blue dispersed, then softly vanished.

A bright green glow traced the border of the hexagonal door. Its six segments divided, and slowly retracted, smoothly gliding into the wall, a huge symmetrical open doorway now ahead of them.

"Hello, I'm Phillip, the Detention Chamber Manager, I'm pleased to meet you all," said a tall, thin man, his voice soft and inviting, which contrasted with his formal shirt and tie. He stood on the opposite side of the opening, his dark-rimmed glasses perched on top of his balding head, and his white shirt, so stiff, it appeared to have been soaked in starch.

He shook each of their hands.

"Just this way", he gestured politely, and the three slowly followed him down a wide, dimly lit corridor.

Phillip removed a plastic card from his trouser pocket, its long keychain trailing from a loop on his waistband, as they approached another massive security door.

He swiped the card on a device on the wall and leant forward to a large, glass screen, resting his chin and forehead onto rubber pads. The eye-scanner cast a vivid green glow, and the pressure door slowly opened with a hiss.

"Here we are, just through here", he said, giving a brisk nod towards a sleek, metallic, AI robot, as it marched down the corridor; its facial recognition scanner hummed as they passed.

"For safety reasons, before we can enter the Vault, I need to bring Sutton's chamber down, this won't take long", he explained, as he stepped towards a window.

Richard and the girls followed, to get a better view.

Through the safety glass they could see row upon row of identical, metal boxes, each chamber a secure prison cell, which were stacked so high, they vanished from sight.

"These are aptly named 'the towers of evil'", said Phillip, as he tapped and swiped the glass.

The glossy surface awoke in a burst of green light and a virtual library of chambers materialised, as he entered his instructions onto the smooth, shiny screen.

The girls watched intently, as chamber 105, on the third row, slowly slid forward, and began to descend on large tracks, situated on the front of the metal casing where it was held. Gradually it lowered to the floor, and traced the track for several more meters, before stopping abruptly.

"Follow me", said Phillip, as they all entered through adjoining, sliding doors.

"Girls, Sutton's restrained inside this chamber in a secure pod, so you'll be quite safe.

He's being held in an induced sleep for your visit, but he'll be awake the next time you meet; you've been watching the AI computer-generated program from what I understand?", Phillip looked to the girls.

Heather and Abbie nodded to confirm.

"So, you're up to speed on his progress, that's good. Sutton's brain readings and thoughts are being monitored constantly, so please be assured, we are in control.

A visual conversion nano–lens has already been programmed and implanted directly to his retinas. The VCN is capable of self-perception and ID morphing", Phillip again, kindly reassured them, as he approached the chamber.

He swiped his card and placed his thumb onto a glowing pad. The locking mechanism slowly rotated and clicked, and the heavy chamber door swung eerily open.

"You are beyond brave, I'm so proud of you both", beamed Richard, as the girls, arms linked, entered the chamber.

3

Jessie had often wondered how Anna had sustained such shocking injuries. She had asked her numerous times about her accident, only to be met with a stoney silence but today, Anna was ready to confide in Jessie, her story…

Anna

"It's been over 2 years now and my life then was almost perfect. I had achieved my dream and qualified as a hair and beauty therapist, shortly before my engagement to Jason, my high-school sweetheart. Sorry, just give me a second", she said, as she grabbed her crutches and headed towards her bed. She picked up a small, white teddy bear, which held a bright-red heart between its arms, then made her way back.

"Did Justin give you the bear, I noticed you often carry it around with you?", asked Jessie.

"His name was *Jason!*", Anna instantly corrected her, clearly annoyed.

"He gave it to me after putting my engagement ring on", she explained sadly.

Jessie glanced at Anna's fingers, which were mutilated, deformed, ugly stubs.

"We were setting up a home together and planning our future. Jason was my rock. I could achieve anything when we were together, I felt indestructible, strong. He was a talented artist, his creativity was amazing, he was going places, but then…"

"Then what?", interrupted Jessie impatiently.

"We began that day. The day our lives changed forever.

Jason had been head-hunted and invited to display his work at the prestigious Marquee-X Art Gallery; he was ecstatic. It was what he yearned to do, to draw and paint. We felt it could have been his lucky break, but we couldn't have been more wrong!".

Anna wiped away the tears which had begun to well, as she bravely continued.

"Jason and I had a few drinks during the day and a girlfriend of mine, whom we bumped into at the exhibit, offered us a ride home.

Travelling back, we were involved in a terrifying incident. I don't remember much, as I was in and out of consciousness. I suffered horrendous injuries, and I couldn't stand the pain, but even through the agony, I witnessed the love of my life die before my eyes. He suffered the most dreadful end; a terrible, slow, agonising death, my sweet Jason", sobbed Anna.

Jessie traced every inch of Anna's face, as she shared her most heartfelt, painful experiences, but she wasn't absorbing her words, but trying to imagine the agony which Anna would have felt, when she had sustained such life-changing injuries.

She was grossly disfigured, with deep scarring around her mouth and eyes. She had large, healed-over holes in her cheeks; a thin layer of skin, almost transparent, stopped the holes from gaping open.

Her jaw jutted slightly to the right, which caused her implanted teeth to sit very awkwardly, their outline visible through the side of her face.

Curls of chestnut-brown hair sat in a chaotic mess on her head, only growing back between the deep-red scarring on her scalp.

Jessie stared at the repulsive, empty socket of Anna's missing brown eye, wondering if she had felt the moment it was torn from her; and had she experienced the pain of her leg being severed from her knee joint?

Jessie again, focussed on Anna's voice.

"…and the unbelievable pain, feeling the remaining shards of tooth fragments slicing through my tongue. I was desperately gasping for breath, as I choked on the blood running down my throat".

There was no doubt, Anna had indeed, suffered greatly.

Suddenly, Jessie felt overwhelmed. Her eyes rolled back into her head, as she sunk into her pillow.

4

Jessie lay motionless.

Drugged. Helpless. Bleeding, and blind.

Cable-ties bound her ankles and wrists, pulled so taught they sliced into her filth-soaked, malnourished limbs.

Layers of brown parcel-tape mummified her head, wrapped so tightly, the contours of her small, pretty face could be traced.

Thin splits in her constraint served as her sole lifeline, enabling her survival from a harrowing, suffocating death.

Her once long, meticulous jet hair had been brutally hacked, exposing her mutilated skull; the glory of her crown now matted, maroon tufts.

Her spinal cord had been severed; a jagged bottle protruded from the arch, its neck surrounded by scarlet, crystal-like fragments, embedded into her bruised, battered body.

She lay contorted and naked, in a mix of congealed blood, and slivers of razor-thin glass.

The refuse truck hovered smoothly to its first pick up, as Jessie lay concealed, and alone.

The robotic arm, with its suction pads active, pivoted outward and gripped a massive array of sparkling bottles and jars. As the arm rotated inward, the vacuum hissed, and a high-pitched alarm beeped, signalling it was ready to release its load.

At that moment, Jessie awoke.

The vacuum silenced, and a chorus of crashing, splintering glass echoed, as the terrified, paralysed teenager; conscious, imprisoned, and powerless, was buried alive, inside a shattered, crystal tomb.

The pistons of the powerful hydraulic press whirred to life, and a massive iron plate descended slowly, ushering in darkness.

A mechanical jaw was preparing for the release of the glass into a transport pod beneath the chassis.

Several AI bots were now poised at their stations, ready to transport the load to the recycling depot.

A hiss of hydraulic steam escaped, and the glass began to yield, then shattered under enormous pressure.

Jessie, on the brink of death, remained helpless, as a prism of crushed glass gushed from the hopper, and scattered into the sealed pod; like a lethal, shimmering-waterfall of daggers.

The container's jaw parted further, as the colossal metal press lowered for the final time.

As its immense weight pressed upon her body, the chute flung open, and Jessie, with no beat of her heart, plummeted into the container.

As the glass dust settled, the protective suction shields lowered and detached.

Jessie lay lifeless, impaled in a shroud of razor thin needles of glass, as the AIs sprang into action, their resuscitation modes now activated.

5

Jessie was desperate to leave Shorelands and had begun to wonder if her memory would ever return.

Mr. Northern, her Brain Surgeon, had explained that her memory loss was a direct result of her accident; tiny bone fragments had splintered and lodged in her brain, resulting in paralysis and acute memory loss.

He went on to say that this had also caused damage to her parietal lobe, which controls pain and senses.

Jessie showed little concern about being numb and unable to feel pain, she was still healing and considered this a blessing.

Mr. Northern had emphasised that it was imperative for Jessie to wear a rapid-heal bandage. The cutting-edge nano-weave dressing clung tightly around her head, airway, and mouth. Her surgeon had explained that it harboured millions of microscopic nanobots, which were engineered to replicate the body's own healing mechanisms; her skin should heal flawlessly, but the process would take several months.

He had promised her that everything, given time, would return to normal, and she would regain all feeling.

She was fortunate, but still felt frustrated. She had so many unanswered questions. *Be patient Jessie, just give it some time*, that was all she seemed to hear.

It was almost 8 months of being bedridden, stifled and confused. She was becoming more annoyed as each day passed.

Though she had no memory of her accident, but for Mr. Northern's explanation of what had happened, she felt she had suffered enough. Her mind would sometimes start rushing, as if at full speed, as it was now.

What is her real name? How did she end up naked in that truck? Why has no one reported her missing or found her? Why haven't the authorities located someone who knows her?

Why?...

"Hi Jess!", called Anna.

"Hi hun!", shouted Holly, interrupting Jessie's thoughts, as the girls returned to the bay.

She hated being referred to as hun or Jess and was beginning to detest the name Jessie, but everyone at Shorelands called her some version or another, but she was unsure why.

"What's wrong, you look fed up?", asked Holly.

"I'm sick of being stuck in here. How can no one have even looked for me, they still have no idea who I am", moaned Jessie.

"The authorities are working tirelessly trying to find out. Give it some time, you may even start remembering details yourself", smiled Holly.

"Yes, I agree", nodded Anna, with a lop-sided grin.

"Good morning how are you feeling today, hun?", called Holly cheerfully, as she threw back her bedclothes.

"What the... What the hell!".

Jessie froze.

"What's going on?", she blurted, her eyes darting, searching the room for answers; a half-eaten bowl of porridge in front of her.

"I don't understand! We were talking a moment ago, it was almost midday! Did I lose consciousness again?".

"I really don't know, I've only just woken up myself", yawned Holly, as she fumbled with an orange head scarf; her attention now shifted away from Jessie, lost in the folds of the fabric.

"Well don't worry about *me* then!", growled Jessie. "Obviously I'm concerned because I keep losing track, everything is so mixed up inside my head. I have no concept of time, one moment it's evening and the next, I'm waking up again!".

"Oh dear, dear, that must be quite frightening, poor you", sympathised Anna.

"Mr. Northern will be on his rounds shortly, you can explain that you're concerned", smiled Holly.

Jessie was so confused. Her thoughts were going off on tangents and she was finding it difficult to focus. She would raise her concerns with her brain surgeon, as it seemed this was the only option available.

Suddenly her mind took off in a different direction, as she watched Holly struggle to lower herself from her bed.

Jessie once asked Anna what had happened to Holly, but she had replied bluntly 'it's not my place to say, if she wanted you to know, she would tell you herself'.

It appeared from Holly's injuries that she had been involved in a fire, or maybe an acid attack. Jessie guessed it must have been some time ago, her scars were healed, but still, there was a rawness to them.

Her skin looked unbearably tight and stretched over her petite frame, and her nose had been ravaged, leaving a deep cavity, with flaps of skin hanging over the shocking sight in places.

She was almost blind in her left eye, which was now a misty, milky white; the pretty aqua blue stripped from it.

The skin on her legs was severely scarred, as though clumps of flesh had been randomly thrown onto the bone, beneath a grafted skin covering.

She had little of her auburn hair, just several long, wispy strands between the scarring on her bright-red scalp; she would often wear a mask, and a scarf tied around her head.

Jessie tried to imagine how painful each movement must be for her.

Suddenly, Jessie's thoughts rebounded back, as Mr. Northern entered the bay. He was dressed in pale green scrubs and white shoes, his grey hair slicked and combed back. He always looked drained, the dark circles beneath his eyes almost black, stress probably, all part-and-parcel of a very demanding position. He looked to be in his late fifties, or maybe slightly older.

"I'm off to the Day Room for a while, see you all later!", shouted Holly, as she shuffled out of the door.

"How are you today Jessie?", asked Mr. Northern, as he pushed back a strand of stray hair, his tall posture slightly hunched, as he walked over.

Jessie shared her concerns with her surgeon, desperate for a logical explanation.

"Don't you fret now, we're monitoring you closely and you probably fainted, your readings seem fine. It's likely you were overcome, as your senses are beginning to return, and you're feeling emotions again".

Jessie was concerned, but at the same time relieved, at finally beginning to feel something, the first time since being admitted to Shorelands.

6

Anna lifted a small, black suitcase onto her bed and started to pack, as Jessie interrupted her.

"Anna, before you leave, would you mind filling me in about that serial killer Garth Sutton, I asked you about him earlier", complained Jessie.

"I already told you briefly when you asked", sighed Anna.

"Oh, I don't remember!", said Jessie, shaking her head.

"I don't want to think about that evil piece of scum, so if you want to know anything you can borrow my VIV, it's all available from the People's Justice Vault, that's where you go to make your judgement count", explained Anna.

"Now you've lost me! What's a VIV and what do we judge?", questioned Jessie, looking confused.

"Oh, of course, you have no idea do you", laughed Anna.

"A VIV is a Vault Information Visor. It resembles a virtual-reality mask if you have any idea what that is! They're simple enough to use. It has a built-in screen with speakers, and a thought processor; you can instruct it simply by thinking.

It also has sensor pads, which sit tightly against your temples, I believe they monitor your pulse, to make sure you're ok", explained Anna.

"What is the Vault?", asked Jessie.

"It's where the convicted criminals' memories are stored. You give the VIV instructions on the file you'd like to view, and it's located within the Vault. Here you can watch their memories and the crimes which they committed; it's as if you're seeing it through the killer's own eyes. It can be very disturbing, to say the least!", shuddered Anna.

"This sounds amazing! So, you can watch their past, as if you were there?", questioned an intrigued Jessie.

"Yes, that's correct, as if you were Garth Sutton himself!", laughed Anna.

"Wow, that sounds fantastic!", said Jessie excitedly, as Anna continued.

"Once you've watched Sutton's files, you can then cast your Judgement vote, which would extend his sentence by one month, if you feel he deserves a longer punishment.

You can also use the VIV to watch any of the PJO's broadcasts. Each file costs 50 credits to view. Surviving victims and their families may receive a percentage of the proceeds raised, under certain circumstances.

It's not just the Sutton case, all the Justice files are available, as well as thousands of crime documentaries and live coverage from Insect Island".

"Insect Island, what's that?", asked Jessie.

"I'll get to that in a moment, first I'll explain what Justice is, I'll use Sutton as an example. The first part of the Justice sentence is a reality T.V. show, which is broadcast for two days, before he receives his Final Justice. The finale takes place in front of a live audience and sometimes includes surviving victims, family members and anyone else who may be involved; it's also available to view on the VIV".

"But I don't have any credits, isn't there another way?", Jessie panicked, already showing an eagerness to discover more.

"Don't worry about the cost, you can use my details. There are more important things in this life than cash, and I receive a very generous yearly allowance. I'll give you my account information when you set up your portal. Just watch a couple of the Sutton files and decide if you'd like to vote, we can sort out the details later", smiled Anna.

"Cheers, that's good of you", said Jessie.

"No problem, it's my pleasure! I know you won't be running away any time soon", she joked.

"Some cases are very disturbing and trust me, once you've seen it, then it's stuck in your brain! Cleansing is expensive, so I won't be able to pay for that", warned Anna.

"Is it painful, having your mind cleansed?".

"No, not at all. Here, I have an information leaflet if you want to take a look?".

"Yes, sure, throw it over", said Jessie eagerly.

MIND RELIEF MARVEL

The low intensity UVA memory extraction dome is a mind cleansing marvel of engineering. This cap is not just a tool but a gateway to a new realm of psychological freedom, offering a chance to erase the scars of the past and emerge anew, and unburden the weight of those unwanted memories.

A seamless dome of polished metal, lined with a soft, biocompatible mesh, is etched with state-of-the-art microscopic circuitry. Thousands of nano-electrodes can map the brain's intricate network of synapses, with unparalleled precision.

The cap's exterior boasts a minimalist elegance, housing technology which is harmonized with the human psyche.

Its quantum processor holds the power to alter human consciousness.

The heart of the system, with quantum algorithms, can isolate and nullify specific memories in minutes, without interrupting core characteristics, personality, or sense of personal history. The subject's fundamental essence will remain, with no disruption to the continuity of the subject's identity.

Relieve your mind with Mind Relief – A safe, pain-free, mind-cleansing experience.

"That sounds interesting", said Jessie.

"I guess so. I'm booked in at the PJO for a session in a couple of weeks, I have flashbacks regularly and I really can't live with them", explained Anna.

"Once you've viewed some of the files, you can then cast your judgement vote. If there are more votes for, than against an extended sentence, then Sutton will serve two months instead of one. It all depends on how many people take the time to visit the Vault, watch the evidence and cast their votes. In a nutshell, the more people who watch and pass judgement, the longer the sentence".

"I understand, but only one month added to a one-month sentence, that doesn't seem much to begin with?", said Jessie, looking confused.

"It may not sound long, but trust me, just sixty seconds of the Justice punishment must seem like an eternity!", shuddered Anna.

"But what happens to them, what *is* the Justice punishment?".

"You'll discover that when Sutton gets what he deserves. I don't want to spoil it for you. I'll make sure you're tuned in, and you can experience that finale feeling for yourself!".

"I'm looking forward to it already", grinned Jessie.

"It's 100 credits to watch the live show, but it's worth every unit! Until you experience The Final Justice it's hard to imagine, but you'll see. Honestly, it's a real mind-twister it truly is, you need a strong mind and a stronger stomach, it really messes with your head".

"Don't worry, I've an iron-clad gut, I'm not squeamish, I would enjoy watching it", laughed Jessie.

Anna scowled.

"There was uproar when the P.J.O first introduced the idea. I believe it was over 6 years before it was agreed it could be trialled.

In the early days, it was nothing like it is now, there was hardly any graphic evidence, and extracting memories was extremely dangerous, but the procedure is completely safe now.

You only hear the news reports, which give you most of the details. The victims and the families often don't disclose their true identities and the court cases are always carried out at a secret location. You decide from the televised information if you think it's worth visiting the Vault. You already know that if they've been sentenced to Justice, then it's going to be extreme.

Some people were also judging the families of the victims, saying that it was immoral allowing their loved one's fate to be shared in such an open way. Others complained that memory extraction was an infringement of human rights.

The PJO was granted the go-ahead to conduct a public vote, which worked in favour of Justice, despite there being some extremely strong protests.

When the first live show was aired it was a phenomenal success, with audience ratings the highest ever in recorded history!".

"I would never tune out", laughed Jessie.

"Well, next came all the other problems which started to arise, and they almost scrapped it for good".

"Why, what happened?", Jessie, for once, was focussed on Anna's every word.

"All the other sickos out there kept revisiting the graphic evidence sites, so that's one thing that had to be stopped".

"Oh, I see, so you can't do that, how come?".

"Once you put on the VIV you look into the screen, and it scans your eyes. It's a pain for me, for obvious reasons; I've spent hours before trying to convince them I'm not a Cyclops from Greek myth", said Anna sadly.

"That's so funny!", laughed Jessie.

"Yes, hilarious isn't it! Anyway, there's a touchpad with a sensor on the side of the visor, where you place your hand and it takes a copy of your fingerprints, which are then kept on the Organisation's files, which has also been a pain for me!".

"Oh yeah, of course", chortled Jessie, glancing at Anna's grotesque hands, which she quickly moved behind her back, away from Jessie's view.

"Lastly, they record your voice and then you're in. You can view the evidence once, but only once, then you're locked out of that file permanently".

Jessie nodded to confirm she understood.

"Anyone trying to record files from the Vault, to make their own sick, private collection would be detected, and sentenced to a visit to the Island".

"So, Insect Island, what is it?", Jessie reminded her.

"It's just what it sounds like. It's an Island concealed under an enormous dome, and its location is unknown. It's overrun with insects, and we're not talking about your average creepy crawlies here. These are massive, mother-of-bugs, which have been scientifically cloned and mutated from normal insects, so they're on a much larger scale and easily capable of killing. Some with stings, some with fangs; spiders the size of a cow! It makes my skin crawl just thinking about that place", she cringed.

"It sounds great! Have you ever seen anyone die there?", asked Jessie, clearly excited.

"Unfortunately, yes. I saw one guy torn-in-two by an enormous death-watch beetle, and a woman impaled through the head by an 8-foot mosquito! It was horrifying. It's the stuff from your nightmares!", winced Anna.

"Oh, wow, I just cannot wait to watch that!", said Jessie eagerly.

"I don't visit there now, it's too gory and graphic for me. There's nothing else on the island. If they want to survive, they need to fend for themselves. Food and water are provided for them, but the bare minimum.

Audience ratings are high for the Island, keeping more funds coming in for the PJO.

Any Law they are convicted of breaking, there is one of three ways to go, depending on the crime committed. For instance, for theft or narcotics, they would be sentenced to Insect Island. If found guilty of rape or paedophilia, then it's The Death Penalty by lethal injection. For first degree murder, they would face their Final Justice.

If there's not enough evidence in cases where it's likely they could be sentenced to death, or they've been found guilty of murder, then a mind sweep is *always* carried out to extract their memories.

Only Justice cases are voted on, and public viewing is only permitted with the express permission of the surviving victims, or families involved", said Anna.

"So, there's never a chance of anyone innocent being convicted?", asked Jessie.

"That's correct. There's no doubt of guilt. In cases of sexual abuse or assault, the evidence is *never* broadcast and would only be available to the jury during the trial".

"Ok, I understand", nodded Jessie.

"Everyone receives a fair trial. Their mental health and family background would be assessed. If convicted, then it's off to the Island, no exceptions. Anyone who manages to survive will have learnt their lesson, trust me, they won't want to go back. If you don't want to face your punishment, then don't break the law!", stamped Anna.

"Bit harsh that!", said Jessie.

"Yes, it is, but it's also effective!

People abide by the New World Law nowadays, because if it's not the Island, you're dead if you're lucky; you do *not* want to face the alternative. Now that the PJO can extract memories, which is irrefutable proof of guilt, and the death penalty is commonplace throughout the world; coupled with the fact that you face Justice if guilty of murder, crime rates have fallen dramatically. Serial killers are few and far between.

Before you can pass Judgement on the accused in Justice cases, you *must* watch the evidence and character files.

These include their background, family upbringing; were they abused as a child.

Garth Sutton is a great example. You've heard the verdict of the court case, the Judge's final statement and Mr. Foster's terrible account of what happened to his daughter, but that's all you know. Would you enter the Vault now to discover the facts and watch Sutton's memories?".

"Absolutely, I would be straight in there!", bubbled Jessie.

"Well, let me make this point crystal-clear for you!

Once you have cast your vote, you are agreeing that he deserves his punishment until the end of an extended sentence".

"Yes, yes, I understand", said Jessie, rolling her eyes.

"You know Jess, maybe we should leave it there, I may have told you way too much already, I'm not sure the doctors would let you…"

"Forget what they would say!", blurted Jessie angrily, and she could see she had taken Anna aback.

"You've suffered trauma to your brain, you know that the mind is very delicate".

"I'll tell them I'm watching a documentary or something, they don't need to know I'm watching anything graphic,", insisted Jessie.

"Ok. You can borrow my VIV now if you're sure", said Anna, as she collected the visor from its charging dock.

"Great, I'm definitely going in!", laughed Jessie, as she eagerly snatched it from her.

"Take a note of my payment details, I think I'll pop to the day room and let you start watching".

"Yeah, ok", nodded Jessie, a pen already eagerly poised.

7

Jessie followed the directions printed on the side of the VIV, put on the visor, and read the onscreen instructions on how to set up her account. She then entered Anna's financial details.

Dramatic music began, as an image of a large set of gold scales stamped onto a black background for several seconds, then faded out.

Words zoomed onto the screen from a distance, in swift succession, growing larger and sharper as they approached; their bright red images still legible after they had vanished.

ABIDE BY THE LAW!

CRIME & PUNISHMENT!

REAP WHAT YOU SOW!

AN EYE FOR AN EYE!

and finally,

JUSTICE!

Images of prisons, an Island and thousands of insects began to appear and slowly fade out from the screen.

"Welcome to The People's Justice Vault", the narrator began.

"Before entering, please listen carefully to the People's Justice Organisation's Terms and Conditions. The disclaimer must be signed before entering. We recommend that people with a nervous disposition…"

Jessie skipped all the T&C's, checked the *I agree to* boxes and looked down the playlist. She eagerly thought the words inside her mind.

'Load, Garth Sutton, Introduction, Play'.

50 credits were automatically deducted from Anna's account, as the narrator began.

"Garth Sutton was born in Maydrift in 2030, a small coastal town located in East Anglacia. He enjoyed a decent upbringing with his mother and father, Joyce and Derek.

Joyce worked as an administrator at a local estate agent, and Derek was a hard-working employee at a construction company.

Sutton had a relatively happy childhood with his younger sister Bella, with no sign of any physical, psychological, or sexual abuse.

He had a strong bond with his father, who left the marital home when Sutton was 13, after a breakdown of the couple's marriage.

Shortly after his father's departure, Joyce and 6-year-old Bella were murdered.

Derek suffered a severe mental breakdown, which tragically resulted in the 42-year-old husband and father taking his own life.

Sutton moved to Marshdown, where he lived with his grandparents.

He did well academically, and at the age of 16 began working at the local police department's post-room, whilst studying to become a junior forensic scientist, progressing to a senior post in less than 9 years.

Employees at the Police Department, where Sutton worked for over 35 years, described him as a private, quiet, intelligent man, who was excellent at his job.

Discover now his mother and sister's true fate and see how they perished at the hands of their trusted brother and son!".

Jessie instructed the VIV.

'*Load, The Joyce and Bella Sutton Murders*'.

Instantly, Jessie was sucked into a wormhole at warp speed, travelling faster than light, drowning in a cesspit of souls. Screaming, grasping, desperate memories clawed at her from every angle. Jessie gulped in air, feeling she was suffocating, adrift within a void of darkness.

Suddenly she was propelled into a spectrum of blinding colour, flashing past at lightning speed. Gradually the bright hues began to fade, as a thick, grey mist formed. Faint images in the distance slowly enlarged and came into focus as the fog began to clear.

She had arrived, now a visitor, transported into the warped mind of a killer.

Jessie was there, on a small fishing boat, with a woman and a young girl, Sutton's mother, and sister.

Jessie was taken aback. She was seeing through Sutton's eyes, the past, his memories.

The surroundings were hazy, as if in a dream.

Sutton was yelling at his mother, as he grasped a rusted, metal fishing-tackle-box in his hand, which was clearly the hand of a youth.

"It's your fault he left, my dad would never have chosen to leave me, you're a filthy, lying whore. He loved me and you drove him away!".

"Son, please, your father was unhappy, he met someone else and that's the reason he's moved away. He still loves you and Bella and I'm sure he'll contact us soon, now please, I don't want to talk about this in front of your sister, she's been through enough!".

"Her! What about me!? You're a fuckin' liar, it's all your fault!", he screamed, his grip on the box handle tightened and his hand began to violently shake.

Suddenly, he raised his arm, letting out a loud 'roar', as he viciously whipped the box around, striking his mother forcefully on her right temple.

She grasped her head for several seconds, as blood began to stream between her trembling fingers.

Slowly, she slumped forward from her seat onto her knees, and collapsed, face-down onto the deck; a deep gulley gouged into her flesh, and her blonde hair, now an ombre scarlet.

It was clear Sutton was panicking, as his eyes were darting frantically around the bow.

Bella's terrified screams rang out, cutting through the silence.

He grabbed a reel of fishing line and turned to face his little sister, shock and terror was reflected in her innocent blue eyes. He roughly gripped her arm and spun the terrified child around, and wrapped the line around her throat, as she struggled, and kicked out in a desperate bid to pull away.

He forced her face down, with a knee pushed firmly into her back and pulled on the line as hard as he could, but her piercing cries for her mummy continued.

He calmly stopped and stepped aside, lifted back his booted foot, and callously kicked her forcefully in the head.

As Bella lay motionless, he returned to the tackle box, which was smothered in his mother's blood, and calmly removed a large knife, which he used for gutting his fish.

As the young girl lay face-down and helpless, her brother straddled her small body, grabbed her long blonde hair, pulled back her head and heartlessly slit her throat.

He stepped away and looked towards his mother, the deck now a ruby lake of blood, and it was clear that she was dead.

He dragged Bella to the side of the boat and coldly tossed her overboard into the ocean. Her small body swayed lifelessly; slowly swallowed into the depths of a cloudy, crimson grave.

Sutton, knife-in-hand, headed towards the corpse of his mother, as the memories began to fade.

Narrator

"Garth Sutton was never questioned in connection to the murders, after his grandparents informed police that their grandson was over 70 miles away, staying at their home in Marshdown at the time it took place".

Jessie slumped back in her bed and let out a breath she hadn't realised she'd been holding.

"Holy shit!", she exclaimed, as she eagerly carried on.

'Load, Donna Lucas, A Close Escape, Play'.

Narrator

"This is a Statement from a girlfriend of the then 21-year-old Sutton.

Donna describes how she almost died during a night at the killer's home. This is her chilling account of the terrifying ordeal".

A fair-haired, middle-aged woman appeared on the screen, her face lined with worry and sorrow, her hazel eyes encircled with darkness.

Visibly shaking, she began her story.

"It was my sixth date with him and even now, over 30 years later, I still cannot bring myself to say his name.

He was an attractive guy, tall and lean, with dark-brown hair and startling blue eyes. He never had a problem attracting women, and I recall feeling lucky he had chosen to see me.

We spent an enjoyable evening at a local club, where we had a few drinks and danced most of the night together. He was attentive, romantic, and made me feel special.

He invited me back to his home for coffee and I was more than happy to go, he was a real gentleman all night and on previous occasions. He even offered to pay for a cab if I would rather leave, which I declined.

He chatted about the house and small fortune his grandparents had left him, after they were killed in a road traffic accident; the brakes in their car had failed.

He confided how distraught he was after the murder of his mother and sister, and the anger he felt towards their killer, who had yet to be caught.

I felt sympathetic towards him, after he shared their terrible fate.

We had both sobered after several coffees. We became intimate and he led me by the hand upstairs to the bedroom.

As I undressed at the foot of the bed, I had my back turned to him, as I was feeling nervous and shy. I removed my clothes and placed them onto a chair at the foot of the bed. He suddenly wrapped my chiffon scarf around my throat, yanking it tightly, choking me. I was terrified. I struggled and clawed at the fabric, when he grabbed my hair and threw me onto my front, pinning me down. I tried desperately to push him off, but he overpowered me and locked his arm tightly around my throat. I was screaming hysterically, when he forced a plastic bag over my head and thrust my face into the pillow. He twisted the bag even tighter, and I couldn't breathe; I truly believed I was going to die! I was about to blackout, when he let out a loud groan, his grip loosened, and his weight fell on top of me. I was frantic and yanked the bag from my head and pushed him off, gasping for breath. He rolled over onto his back; I knelt backwards in shock, unable to stop shaking.

He suddenly sat up and put his hand over my face and shoved me hard across the bed; my head smashed into the bedside table.

He shouted at me to '*Fuck off, you're just a filthy slut like my mother!*'.

Naked, I grabbed his shirt from the chair and ran towards the door, but he instantly sprang from the bed and pinned me violently against the wall. He clamped his hand around my throat, and I will never forget how he looked at me, I knew, the words he was about to speak he truly meant.

He warned me, '*If you speak of this to anyone, breathe a word to a soul, then it will be the last breath you ever take! I swear, I will hunt you down, rip out your eyes, and cut out your fuckin' heart!*'.

I fled for my life. I had never, or since been more petrified than I was that night.

My biggest regret is not finding the courage to come forward sooner. I have lived in fear, and I want him to suffer. He should pay for as long as possible for murdering those poor, innocent people.

Please vote, he deserves to rot!'".

Suddenly, the bay doors opened, and in walked Anna and Holly, much to Jessie's annoyance.

"You're not still watching it are you? I stopped after poor little Bella, I couldn't stomach anything else, and that was more than enough to deserve my vote!", stamped Holly.

"I never made it any further either", shuddered Anna.

"Well, I've only really listened to the introduction and signed all the bumf, I haven't seen any of Sutton's memory files yet", lied Jessie. "I was going to watch some more, but maybe later".

"Come on Anna, do you fancy going to the entertainment suite, we could catch the evening movie and try to forget about that sick piece of crap?", asked Holly.

"Yes, let's go and leave her to it!".

"Bye then", said Jessie eagerly, already back in the Vault.

8

Jessie awoke early before the lights were on and instantly grabbed the visor, to be greeted by a bright red screen, with white, bold flashing words reading 'low battery'. Disappointed, she stared at the charging dock on Anna's bedside table.

"Odyssey, self-navigation wheelchair, bay 1", she instructed, but as usual, no chair arrived, leaving her seething.

Unable to leave her bed she waited impatiently.

Over an hour later she felt she would boil over, annoyed that the girls were still sleeping. She lay swearing to herself for several more minutes, until a blanket of fluorescent light pulsed across the ceiling. The large window at the back of the room burst into brightness, as an animated galaxy of stars scattered, and a kaleidoscope of dusty colours dissolved, replaced with a fresh, green forest, flooded with morning sunshine.

"At last!", shouted Jessie.

"Yeah, morning", yawned Holly, whilst Anna sat herself up in bed.

"I need the VIV charging!", Jessie blurted her demand.

"Wow, can I at least open my eye!", snapped Anna.

"You're eager", said Holly, as she placed a short, auburn wig onto her head.

"How far have you got on the Sutton case, have you voted yet?", she asked Jessie.

"No, not yet. I'd like to see a couple more of his memories, so that I can make an informed decision".

"Hun, really, how many times do you need to see the guy slaughter someone to decide! Get on with it and cast your vote!", snapped Holly.

"Yes, ok, ok, keep your wig on!", barked Jessie cruelly.

"I've already decided that I'll vote. I cannot wait to see him suffer!", chortled Jessie.

"No, neither can we", said Anna, and they all broke out into fits of laughter.

Nurse Andrews entered the bay and made her way to a linen cupboard at the back of the room. Jessie watched her intently, as she often did.

She was tall and slim, with ash-grey hair tied into a neat bun. Jessie had noticed on many occasions her stunning green eyes. She wore a navy dress, which was tight and stretched across her ample bust, with dark stockings and flat black shoes; she always appeared smart and well presented. Jessie admired her shapely legs, and noticed how her tight uniform hugged her bottom.

Anna interrupted her stare.

"Not on the VIV yet Jess?", she shouted sarcastically.

"No, the battery is dead", snapped Jessie, scowling back.

"Nurse, would you mind passing Jess the charging dock", smirked Anna, as though deliberately trying to make her aware of Jessie's visits to the Vault.

"Yes, of course, no problem", smiled the nurse.

"Give it 5 minutes Jessie, it doesn't take long. Be careful what you choose to watch, we don't want you seeing anything which could set back your recovery", she warned her, and sat the charging dock onto the table.

"I'm only watching documentaries… honestly!", lied Jessie, and placed the visor onto the dock.

"Good. See you all soon!", smiled the nurse, as she left.

"Hun, why don't you vote on the Sutton case now, we wouldn't want you having the VIV confiscated!", Holly warned her, giving a sideward nod towards Anna. "We have an idea, so, get that out of the way, and we can concentrate on you", she smiled kindly.

"Yes, ok, you're right", agreed Jessie, throwing Anna a scowl, and several minutes later cast her judgement vote.

"Well done Jess, you've made the right decision", grinned Anna, as Holly beamed back.

"Come on, it's time. Are you sure you're ready?", Anna asked with concern.

"Absolutely, I'm more than ready!", said Holly.

"Jess, we were wondering, would you like to do your hair and nails as it's shower day and you can finally get that bandage removed. Mr. Northern said it would be fine for you to have a make-over, it may even stir up some memories!", smiled Anna.

"A make-over, me! You must be joking!", laughed Jessie hysterically.

"Oh, come on Jess, I have all the gear from when I qualified as a beautician, you're more than welcome to use anything you like", offered Anna.

"I've already said no! I'm not into make-up or any of that crap!", growled Jessie.

Holly shuffled over to Jessie and spoke softly.

"Listen, this is the first time Anna has mentioned her beauty therapy since…well, you know about Jason, just do it for her, even if you don't want to. It sounds like she's ready to take back her VIV. Do this one, simple thing. Just imagine if you could no longer visit the Vault!".

Jessie detested the idea, but knew she had no choice but to agree. She couldn't risk losing the VIV.

"Just get on with it then!", fumed Jessie.

"Ok, let's do this!", said an excited Holly.

"Brilliant!", squealed Anna, as she walked over to her bed, picked up a large, black leather bag and struggled back to Jessie.

"I have loads of nail varnishes in here, help yourself", she said, as she dropped the heavy bag onto Jessie's bed.

"Wonderful", snarled Jessie sarcastically.

"This cosmic purple is lovely, use this one hun, it would suit you", said Holly, as she passed it over.

"Yes, yes okay, whatever", sighed Jessie, and begrudgingly snatched it from her.

She removed the lid and began to paint the dark varnish onto her thumb, as both girls attentively stood and watched, and continued watching, until each nail was covered.

"That's lovely, such an improvement, don't you think so Anna?", said Holly, still staring at Jessie's hands.

"It looks bloody fantastic!", shouted Anna, and both girls began to snigger.

"What's so funny!", snapped Jessie, but they just ignored her.

Suddenly, Nurse Andrews returned, closely followed by a self-navigation wheelchair.

Jessie had been looking forward to being unhooked from her brain monitor, and she would finally have her suffocating bandages removed.

"Oh, your nails do look nice, don't they girls. What colour is that, scarlet?", asked the nurse.

"No, it's purple!", Jessie corrected her, wondering how she could possibly confuse the two.

"Oh, it has a red tinge to it, it suits you though!", smiled the nurse.

"Come on then, let's get you smelling a bit more pleasant! I believe Mr. Northern has some news for you", said the nurse, as she removed the pads attached to Jessie's temples.

"What news, what is it, just tell me now!", demanded Jessie.

"Now, now, temper, temper. I'm not sure, and he's on his rounds for a couple more hours. Don't worry, you're not going anywhere are you, he'll get around to you soon enough".

Jessie tutted and grunted, as the nurse yanked her from the bed and let her drop into the wheelchair.

"Odyssey, self-nav wheelchair 1, destination Shower Room", instructed Nurse Andrews, and the wheelchair slowly manoeuvred its way from the bay.

Jessie was transported down a long, white corridor, the lights almost blinding, as she entered the only room, situated on the right.

She struggled to remove her gown, and the nurse attached a safety harness to the chair, lifted it over Jessie's head, and clipped it into place.

"Here's the remote. Don't set it too hot now, we wouldn't want you burning that lovely skin! You have such a nice complexion now Jessie, it's amazing how you've healed so quickly and flawlessly. I'm sure the girls would give anything for skin like yours, wouldn't they?".

"Yes, I'm sure they would, you've seen the state of the two of them!", said Jessie cruelly, sick of getting no sympathy for her own suffering.

"Well, they're extremely brave girls with what they've been through and how they're coping, a real inspiration!", stamped the nurse.

"I've been through a lot too! I can't even get out of that bed! I've drains and tubes stuck in all sorts of places, and these bandages suffocating me for months!", whined Jessie.

"Oh, of course, poor, poor you. You truly have suffered, haven't you sweetheart".

Jessie again felt the same lack of sincerity in Nurse Andrews words.

"You can remove the bandages yourself, just make sure they're nice and wet before taking them off. Press the buzzer when you're finished. Enjoy", said the nurse, as she slammed the shower room doors behind her.

***

When Jessie returned to the bay over an hour later, the girls were on Anna's bed whispering and sniggering.

Nurse Andrews pressed a button on the back of the wheelchair, and its seat elevated, and arms lowered, and Jessie slid herself back onto her bed – yet again hooked-up to the brain monitor.

"How does it feel to finally see who Jessie is", smiled the nurse. "Have those big, blue eyes stirred up any memories yet?".

"No, nothing. I don't recognise myself at all!", sighed Jessie.

"Oh, that's a terrible shame. I'm sure you'll remember soon", sympathised the nurse, "I'll leave you girls to it, see you all later", she said, as she left.

"Oh, my goodness… look at your skin, it's glowing", Holly complimented her.

Jessie did feel much better, although the water temperature didn't warm her skin, no matter how high the setting.

"Make-up time!", exclaimed Anna.

"Oh no! No way! I am *not* putting any slap on, you can forget that!", raged Jessie angrily.

"Come on hun, you promised. If not for us, do it for your beloved VIV", smirked Holly.

"Just get on with it then!", snarled Jessie.

"Here", said Anna, as she lobbed a blusher and eyeshadow set onto Jessie's lap, followed by a large brush.

"Just a bit of rouge and some eye shadow, we just want you to look your best", she said, giving her a broad grin.

Jessie picked up the brush and loaded it with bronzing colour and applied it to both cheeks. She continued with a pale green shadow on her eyelids.

"There, happy now!", she snapped, glaring at the girls.

"Oh my!", gasped Anna, as Holly squeezed her hand and looked away.

"I told you I've no idea how to put slap on! What's wrong with you?".

"You just look so, so…hot, such an improvement!", said Anna.

"Just some lippy and you're done," said Holly, throwing Jessie a pale pink lipstick.

"Oh, for crying out loud. There, happy now!", she ranted angrily after applying it.

"Oh yes, perfect! It's melted years off you, don't you think so Holly?", sniggered Anna, giving her a gentle nudge.

"Yes. Breathtaking", laughed Holly.

"You will love this Jess, I have this hairdryer, you can have a blow-dry. It must feel lovely having washed that greasy mop. Give it a good blast with this. I envy you having such lovely hair", Anna complimented her.

"Yes ok, why not!", agreed Jessie, as she snatched the dryer and turned it on.

"It feels a bit cold, is there a heat setting on it?", she shouted, as she aimed the nozzle at the top of her head, shaking it around to dry her short, dark hair.

"Oh no, I can't look!", said Anna, as the girls tried to watch.

"What did you say, I missed that?", shouted Jessie over the high-pitched noise of the dryer.

"Oh, nothing hun, nothing at all!", Holly shouted back.

"How does that look?", asked Jessie.

"You look scorching hot!", grinned Anna.

"Oh, you're so good at this!", laughed Holly.

"What the fuck is that supposed to mean, and why do you keep laughing?", raged Jessie, having had her fill of their sarcastic comments, and never sharing why everything was *so* amusing.

"I'm not sure what you mean. We weren't laughing at you, we weren't laughing at all!", Holly assured her, sincerity clear in her voice.

"I'm not stupid! I know what I can see and hear!", shouted Jessie.

"Jess, I'm so worried about you. You're imagining things", said a concerned Anna.

"Will you stop fuckin' calling me Jess!!".

"Please, please, calm down! We didn't mean to upset you, that's the last thing we would do. We're all friends, remember?", pleaded Anna.

Jessie could feel herself becoming more confused around the girls as the days passed and now with Nurse Andrews too.

"Try not to worry, everything will be ok", smiled Anna kindly, as she offered her the VIV. "Why don't you watch something on here, it might take your mind off things?".

"Yes, ok, I will do after some sleep", said Jessie, as she settled herself into her bed and closed her eyes, as the girls stood staring, and continued staring, until they finally turned away, hand in hand.

9

Jessie awoke to total darkness, the bay quiet and empty. She thought it strange that the lights were off and turned on her nightlight, noticing that the girl's beds were neatly made. *Maybe they've gone home already,* she thought.

She grabbed the visor and entered the Vault.

'Insect Island', she instructed.

"Please wait to be connected to the next available live broadcast…"

"Oh, bloody marvellous!", she moaned, and impatiently waited.

***

The Vault, Rehabilitation Facility

"We have a few reoffenders in today Steve, pods 32 to 58, they're gluttons for punishment some of these idiots!", laughed Max.

"Yeah, aren't they just! It looks like that's all of them for now, so I'll double-check the airlines and restraints", said Steve.

"I think pod number 39 could do with a tweak, could you adjust the air pressure in the pads Max, she's a big girl, but there's still room for movement".

Max stood at a large, crystal computer screen. The muddle of confusing symbols would mean nothing to the untrained eye.

He began to tap the glossy screen, its appearance somewhat deceptive, one-touch and you would believe it would dissipate, like wafting a misty wall of smoke.

The cushioned sides surrounding the woman began to inflate, moulding around her body, and once she was securely held and fixed in place, the airflow cut off automatically.

The pods were suspended vertically, attached to a large conveyor-like beam – the cases resembling an open casket hung in a slaughterhouse.

Max continued with his tapping and swiping, almost frantic. *'He looked like a demented orchestra conductor'*, Steve had once joked.

The white, glossy pods began to descend, with the unconscious prisoners inside, held tightly in a standing, soldier-like pose.

"Ok, allocate the viewers please, then we can get things going", said Steve.

"I've already sent the uploads; they're set to be activated when you give me the nod. This is my least favourite part, I don't understand why we must run this file?", complained Max.

"Well, it's all part of rehab' and the deterrent, that's why the PJO want the audience to see it, they must believe that this would happen to them if they were ever convicted and find themselves in the same situation.

Also, many viewers are curious to know *how*, so it's also an explanation", said Steve.

"Yes, but as a viewer, it would freak me out!", shuddered Max.

"Well, that goes to prove it's having the right effect. Let's get it done, time for your next concerto!", joked Steve.

Max pressed a red button on the front of each pod, which activated a mesh-like mask from the side of the prisoners' heads, which moulded snugly over their faces.

A transparent-domed lid at the rear of each pod encircled around to the front; a gush of steamy vapour hissed, and the lights turned green, the caskets now sealed airtight.

The crystal on the computer screen lit up, each prisoner now a numbered image on the monitor, their vital signs quietly beeping away.

A pale mist began to fill each pod, as the occupants continued their slumber.

"The uploads are complete, can I connect the viewers now?", asked Max, as Steve made his way behind the computer.

"Just give me a moment for authorisation", he said, as he entered a long code onto a touchpad. "Ok, all set, time to get them acquainted. Do you fancy a cuppa?".

"Yeah, go on then, cheers mate", said Max, his hands clasped behind the back of his head, as he tilted back his chair, observing bright lines and intermittent peaks of vital signs.

10

"Finally!", Jessie whinged, as her screen flickered on.

Rows of small mugshots began to appear on her screen. They scrolled and shuffled, until she could no longer focus on their details, then stopped abruptly, and a photograph of a man loaded.

He had a tanned complexion, deep brown eyes and dark-brown hair, which was close shaven. A hint of stubble shadowed his jawline and he looked to be in his mid-thirties.

A woman's voice could be heard, talking very matter-of-factly.

"You have been randomly allocated Prisoner-Number: 135-672-049, David O'Connor, who is serving a 72-hour sentence.

You will now be redirected to the People's Justice Rehabilitation Vault, where you will see your prisoner being prepared for dispatch to the island. Please be patient as you are transferred to the R.V. facility. Connection to their eye-camera may take several minutes".

"What is this, it's not insect island and what's going on with this crappy visor, I can't see anything now!", moaned Jessie, tapping the side of the VIV.

Suddenly she was connected.

She cried out and gasped, as a long needle slowly retracted from her eyeball!

"What the hell!", she shouted, as she grabbed at the front of the visor in an attempt to escape the needle's sharp point, the hollow shaft magnified, as she stared down its length.

Slowly the mechanical arm wielding the syringe glided away, its control smooth and methodical.

Jessie worked out she was standing, encased inside a long, oval container. Her stare was fixed ahead, looking into a huge room. Large air vents were visible, fitted into cold, grey steel walls.

She could hear a man's voice moaning and realised what was happening, she was seeing through David O'Connor's eyes and could hear him clearly.

She was now a spectator, observing through his eye-cam.

His moans grew louder, and she could see he was trying to struggle but unable to move.

The woman's voice continued.

"Please remain calm. You are about to be placed into an induced deep-sleep ready for transportation to the island, breathe normally through your mask. You may experience a cold sensation, as your pod fills with gel, which will set within 10-15 seconds, dependant on your body temperature.

Please try not to panic. In the unlikely event any gel is swallowed, it is non-toxic and will safely dissipate.

This procedure is totally painless and completely safe, so please, try to relax. You will arrive on the island within 1 hour of sleep activation".

Jessie could hear O'Connor gasping and holding his breath, as he desperately tried to raise his head, but to no avail.

She sensed his terror through his murmured screams, as a thick, midnight-blue gel began to engulf his eyes.

As his humming became louder and the brightness from the computer screen slowly began to fade, Jessie, again, was left in darkness.

She impatiently waited, when her screen suddenly flashed with the dreaded low battery warning and her visor turned off instantly.

"No way, you have got to be kidding me!", she ranted, as she pulled off the VIV and scanned the room for the charger, which Anna had deliberately moved and left on her bed.

She pressed the alarm button, without releasing her finger for several minutes, but no one appeared.

"Bastards!", she ranted, fuming that no one had rushed to help her.

She placed the visor on again, desperately hoping it may have miraculously charged itself. Disappointed, she yanked it off.

She was taken aback, as dazzling sunshine poured into the bay.

"What the… it's happened again!".

"What has?", asked Holly, as she made her way over, looking concerned.

"It was night-time just a moment ago, it was dark, and no one was here. I don't understand how I can be losing so much time!". Jessie looked to Holly, her eyes desperately searching for answers.

"It's probably all those visits to the vault messing with your head!", suggested Anna sarcastically.

"Can it do that?", Jessie was desperate to find out the cause.

"No idea. Maybe?", shrugged Anna.

"I wouldn't worry too much, if there was a serious problem they would know, your monitor readings would tell them", smiled Holly.

"Well, yes, I suppose that's right, they must be keeping me wired up here for a good reason", calmed Jessie.

"It's probably something and nothing. Try and forget about it for now", said Holly.

"I hope you're right! I was about to enter Insect Island, but the visor died".

"Here, I'll fetch the dock for you, and you can use my charging cable, it will work whilst it charges", said Holly.

"Oh, great, now you tell me! I can get straight back in there then!", grinned Jessie.

"How far had you got, had they linked you to a prisoner yet?", asked Anna.

"Yes. I totally freaked out when they pulled the needle out of his eye", laughed Jessie.

"You should still be connected to the same person until their sentence ends, or they flat-line, whichever comes first", explained Anna.

"There, you can use it now, it's plugged in", smiled Holly.

"Great!", said Jessie, already with the visor on.

Connection Lost, the message flashed repeatedly.

"I don't believe it, it won't connect!", she fumed, as she continued repeating her commands.

"Just give it some time Jess, it can be temperamental occasionally", explained Anna.

"Bloody wonderful!", whined Jessie, as she continued trying.

11

"Welcome to Insect Island"

"Finally! It had better be worth the wait, that's all I can say!", moaned Jessie.

"Please be aware before viewing that the following content may be of an extremely violent, graphic nature, and could also contain scenes of suffering and death. You may leave the island at any time, simply use the 'exit' command to return to the home menu. You will now be reconnected".

Jessie suddenly felt as though she was falling, dropping from the sky like an express train hurtling towards the ground, a cloudy, white mist flashing past her. Gradually the speed began to decline and a grey static on her screen stopped fuzzing and began to focus.

She could hear David O'Connor's heavy breathing, as branches snapped, and dry leaves crunched beneath his feet.

He clambered over a thin, twisted-tree-trunk that had blocked his path through the dense, dark forest.

"Don't look back, just keep running Ellie!", he yelled as he turned back, to see Ellie had fallen face down in the mud.

She was clawing at the ground and all around her, desperately trying to find something to grasp to pull herself to her feet.

"Get up. Get up now, they're right on our arses!", hollered David.

"Just go, leave me here!", cried Ellie, as she tried to push herself to her feet, but slipped back in thick-black sludge, as though trying to run on an oiled surface, her strength leaving her.

She lay face down, caked in dirt and sweat, on the verge of exhaustion.

David could see her fight and hope fading.

"Don't you fuckin' give up, you have got to keep going! Come on Ells, we will soon be out of here, get up, now!", he barked.

David rushed back and grabbed the sleeve of her filthy camouflage jacket and dragged her along in the mud, until she clambered and regained her footing.

"I just can't go any further, I can't do it!", she sobbed, falling to her knees.

David yanked her to her feet, shaking her roughly, as her body flopped like a limp ragdoll.

"They're coming. Do you want to fuckin' die! Come on Ellie, you can do this, I know you can!".

Ellie stared at the ground, as tears streamed down her face.

"For fuck's sake, pull yourself together!", he boomed at her.

"Ok. Ok, don't shout at me!", her words were almost inaudible through the sobs, as she wiped her filthy hand over her face.

"Come on, you can do it!", said David, and dragged her firmly by the hand behind him.

"What insects are they, did you see them?", Ellie panted, tree branches ripping through her torn clothes.

"You really want to know?", he asked in a whisper.

He continued towards a shaft of light breaking through the darkness, discarding a large spear he had painstakingly whittled, which was now hindering their speed.

"Oh, wait. No. Why did you do that!", screeched Ellie, as she watched their only weapon being engulfed into thick sludge.

"It's not going to help us. Just keep running, we need to make it to the river, it's our only chance!", said David, as his pace quickened.

Ellie began to wheeze and struggled to catch her breath, the mud now a thick, crackled mask on her pale skin.

She pushed her short, auburn, crusty hair away from her tired hazel eyes, as they reached the border of the forest.

"Come on, we need to keep moving!", ordered David, as he held back the jagged branches.

Ellie pushed herself through the opening, letting out a piercing cry, as razor-sharp thorns slashed her palm, leaving a gaping wound, pouring with blood.

"Don't worry, it's ok", said David, trying to calm her down, and tore a long strip of material from his t-shirt and gently wrapped it around her hand.

"It isn't far now. Don't stop, keep running, it sounds like an army".

"My God, not the leafcutters, please, tell me it's not them!", she cried.

"Just keep going Ells, we can do this. They may follow us into the river, they can float, but we have a better chance in water than on land".

They were now in open grassland, trying to muster the little energy they had left, knowing they were running for their lives.

The terrifying beat of the ants' chase was gradually becoming louder, as David yanked her to a stop. "Let's catch our breath for a moment, or we aren't going to make it".

"How many are there?", panted Ellie.

"I'm not sure, maybe twenty or so", said David, as he bent over, his hands on his thighs, trying to catch his breath.

He had researched the bugs since his last visit to the island.

The leafcutter ants were roughly shoulder height to a human. Their exoskeleton was like a suit of armour, totally solid, and incredibly strong.

They had mandibles like shears, resembling two razor sharp, serrated kitchen knives, which can crush and slice with ease.

David knew if the ants caught up with them, they would never survive.

"Time to go!", he ordered.

They began to run, which quickly turned into a sluggish jog and then a paced walk, unable to dig up the strength to go any faster.

"Here!", he hollered, as he dragged Ellie towards a small, moss-covered, rock formation, the sound of the river now within earshot.

"Be careful, it's slippery", he warned, as she took his hand, and they made their way safely over the craggy rocks.

David looked back towards the forest.

"Oh shit. Ellie, look!", he exclaimed, as he grabbed her by the shoulders and spun her around.

Not far in the distance were 3 men, desperately sprinting away, the army's hunt now averted from Ellie and David.

The ants, fast and powerful, caught them within seconds.

Ellie closed her eyes tightly and placed her hands over her ears.

David stared, the low, setting sun dazzling his eyes. He watched intently, as the insects swiftly crushed and dissected their prey.

Their chilling screams echoed, as limbs were thrown into the air and tumbled to the ground, the fresh green-grass now a deceptive, attractive illusion of a field of blood-red poppies.

David waited until the slaughter was over and the shrill cries finally stopped.

"Poor bastards", he whispered.

He tapped Ellie on the shoulder, and she almost jumped out of her skin, as he gently removed her hands from her ears.

"It's ok, you can open your eyes now", he said softly.

"I don't understand how you can watch, it's just so awful, the things that happen here", shivered Ellie, the warmth of the day now being blown away by the cool, late-evening breeze.

"I must see it and deal with the horror, it's the best way to become strong. I must survive and get out of here! Come on, we need to keep moving, it will be dark soon. I know where the pick-up point is, we should make it in plenty of time. Are you strong enough to walk, we've lost the ants now?", he asked, concerned Ellie may feel as bad as she looked.

"I'm not sure, I'm so weak and feel sick", she winced.

"It's ok, look, just sit down, rest here for a while", he said, as he took a small hip flask from his trouser pocket.

"Here, take-a-sip".

Ellie grabbed the flask, her filthy hands shook wildly, as she took a huge gulp.

"Whoa, easy there!", he panicked, and snatched the container from her.

"I'm so tired, I just want to go home", cried Ellie, her tears leaving tracks down her pretty face.

"How did a young girl like you end up on Insect Island, how old are you?".

"I'm 23. I'm here for attempted drug smuggling. I worked at an airline, for the department in control of human remains. Another employee and I tried to conceal cocaine inside a coffin, and we were caught, well, obviously, otherwise I wouldn't be here".

She looked to the ground, shifting a small stone around with her foot, wiping her dripping nose on her cuff.

"Well, you are paying the price now. Let this be a valuable, last lesson for us both!", said David, as he tried to lift her spirits.

"I thought this was your second visit to the Island?", Ellie quizzed him.

"Yes, it is, but I've learnt my lesson this time around, trust me, I don't want to die here!".

Ellie bent over, a hand on each knee, her head slumped and back arched, as she began to retch several times, then threw-up bright-yellow bile, which splattered all over David's black boots.

"Oh, I'm so sorry!".

"It's ok, don't worry about it, I think a bit of puke is the least of my problems!", he quipped, as he smiled and gently rubbed her back.

Ellie straightened up and wiped her face, as she began to calm.

"I want to thank you David, for saving me yesterday. If you hadn't come along and helped me, I doubt I'd be alive right now!".

"There's no need to thank me, anyone would have done the same", he smiled.

"I would never have been able to get myself out of that swamp and I can imagine I'd have suffered an unpleasant end. What the hell were those things anyway?".

"They were some sort of leech. I'd say they were hundreds of times larger than a normal one. Their underside looked like some sort of Venus flytrap, I've never seen anything like it before", he said.

Ellie shivered, but this time at the thought of her fate, had it not been for David's bravery.

"It makes you wonder, doesn't it?", he asked.

"What does?".

"Well, what sort of sick fuckers engineer all these mutant insects and create the different habitats on the island, they must be total sadists!", laughed David, as he stamped his foot and wiped his boot on a patch of grass on the riverbank.

"We have to go now", he said, as dusk brought darkness and a cutting chill.

"We will walk along the bank; the river's current is quite strong and flowing in our favour. If you see anything Ellie jump, don't stall! I know the cold is our biggest problem, but we have more chance of surviving hypothermia than a bug; we don't have long until we're transported back", he reminded her, and she nodded. "Just remember, if you do end up in the river, let it do the work for you. We *are* going to make it!", he promised.

Ellie smiled, her teeth a brilliant white against the thick dirt on her face.

"Oh, my hand!", she gasped, as blood dripped onto the muddy bank.

"It's ok, you'll be fine, come on, let's get a move…"

Suddenly the ground sprang open!

Jessie jumped, as 8 huge, black-glazed eyes flashed past her screen.

Thick, branch-like legs grabbed Ellie around her torso, her arms pinned to her side.

Her piercing screams echoed.

"David, help me, help me!", she shrieked, and he frantically tried to pull her away.

"Ellie! Ells! Noooo!", he wailed, as he viciously punched, kicked, and clawed at the enormous spider, desperately trying to break its vice-like grip.

Jessie could hear the crunching and cracking of Ellie's bones over her high-pitched chilling screams, as the spider crushed her body like a paper bag. Her eyes almost bulged out, as thick, syrup-like blood bubbled and splattered from her mouth. Shards of bone pierced through her upper-arm, as she writhed in agony, the sound of her snapping ribs almost drowned out by her blood-curdling howls. Enormous fangs plunged into her shoulder, thrusting in-and-out, and as if attached to an elastic rope, the bristle-like brown spider sprang back, as it dragged Ellie to its nest. A screech of pain resounded, as her spine snapped, and she was folded almost in two. She disappeared, pulled beneath the ground into its burrow, the trap-door slamming shut behind them.

David collapsed onto his knees, still bawling out her name.

"Holy crap, that was brilliant!", squealed Jessie.

Suddenly the darkness changed to a grey fuzz, with the dreaded message, '*connection lost*'.

"Oh, you have got to be kidding me!", raged Jessie, angrily pulling off the visor and throwing it onto her bed, totally oblivious of Anna watching her.

"What's wrong Jess?", asked Anna, as she made her way over.

"I've been bloody cut off again, it was just getting really good too!", she ranted.

"What were you watching?".

"Some girl being dragged into a spider's nest. I didn't see what happened to the guy, I'll never know now if he survives!".

"It sounds like you were lucky being cut-off, I bet that would have been an awful sight", shuddered Anna.

"No way, I loved it! I'll keep trying, maybe I can get it working again", said Jessie hopefully.

Anna shook her head and walked over to the front of the room.

"Odyssey, load the PJO News Channel", she said, and the crystal screen burst into light.

"There's a debate on shortly regarding Justice if you're interested", said Anna.

"I'm going to see if I can get reconnected, and if not, I may watch it".

"I'll just leave the television on then".

"Yeah, cheers", said Jessie, from behind the visor.

12

<u>The Vault, Rehabilitation Facility</u>

Max yawned, as he traced the glow of beats across his screen, like a rhythmic, calming lullaby, and his eyes began to close.

"Oiii!", shouted Steve, as he slapped the back of Max's head, making him lunge forward in his chair and instantly straighten from his slouch.

"Here's your tea. Sorry I was a while, you almost ended up with soup, that machine's useless!", said Steve, placing a cup onto the workstation. "You were nodding off then!", he laughed.

"I never nod off!", said Max clearing his throat, as he levered himself up, pushing against the chair arms.

"No, of course not", joked Steve, as he scanned the screen.

"Pod number 43 has almost completed stage two; the rest aren't far behind. David O'Connor, which file was he given?".

"Hang on one moment", said Max, as he tapped the screen. "Ah, one of the trapdoor spiders, my most feared, I'm a total arachnophobe!", he cringed.

"Oh, no way, that one I would probably request! If they were real, mine would have to be the common housefly. Those nasty little shites lay their eggs under the skin. The larvae hatch into maggots, which crawl beneath the surface, feeding on the flesh. When they're ready to escape, they regurgitate acidic saliva from their stomach and burn their way from the inside out. Now seeing someone endure that, my friend, is truly horrific!", shivered Steve, as he rubbed his hand up and down his arm.

"Mind you, none of them are pleasant", laughed Max.

"Well, they're not supposed to be, are they! So, this O'Connor, is he at the pick-up point, how much of the file is left to run?".

"Oh, yup, he's almost ready, only a couple of minutes of the file to go", nodded Max.

"That's all levels almost complete, so they can be shuttled down to the Recovery Vault as soon as their files end. With a bit of luck, they will have learnt their lesson. Don't you find it hard to believe that the prisoners take it all in so willingly?", asked Steve.

"What do you mean?", asked Max, looking puzzled.

"Well, right from the start. I know what they experience looks and feels real, but still, they're so quick to accept it all, surely you would question it. I know I would in that situation", said Steve.

"I would just be relieved I survived! There's no reason to think it's not reality. You would have a harder time trying to convince me that it wasn't real! It could be, because you're privy to the truth, that you think you'd work it out?", suggested Max.

"Yes, maybe you're right. I know some of the public believe the island to be *the devil's work* but if they knew the truth, that it doesn't exist, and all deaths are computer-generated, then their opinions would probably change", added Steve.

"Yes, well, they will never know because if they did, then rehab' just wouldn't work", said Max.

"These level two prisoners won't be given a third chance; they break the law again then it's the death penalty! It's rare to get many of those after going through rehab", said Steve.

"Statistics show that most people after their first visit to rehabilitation are reformed characters, they don't commit further offences, so it certainly seems to work!", agreed Max.

Steve nodded. "How's everyone doing, stats all good?".

"Yup, all files are now complete, an easy one today, no problems at all", smiled Max.

"Great. Let's get this batch sent off to the Recovery Vault", said Steve.

Max entered his instructions, and the transportation rail lowered, each pod clipping itself securely onto the beam.

The beam rose, and like a cascade of synchronised waves, the pods smoothly traced the sleek track, until they vanished through a hatch in the top, far corner of the Rehab Vault.

"That's the notification sent to Recovery that they're on their way", said Max, giving Steve a thumbs up.

"If we shuttle in the next prisoners, maybe we can get an early finish before shift change-over!", grinned Steve.

"That sounds good to me buddy", smiled Max.

13

God versus Justice

"Good evening, I'm Russel Cameron and welcome to, 'Your World - Your Say'.

Tonight's topic for debate, once again, is the controversial organisation, The People's Justice.

The Global Crime Index now stands at a mere 0.5%, an unprecedented testament to the effectiveness of the New World Law.

Since its introduction and with the People's Justice Organisation in place, more than ten-fold of the guilty are being rehabilitated, executed, or in extreme cases, sentenced to Justice.

Conviction statistics in the last ten years have dropped dramatically, a clear indication that the system is swiftly having a positive effect, bringing about a safer environment in which we can all live.

Financial comparisons are also in favour of the Organisation, the taxpayer now free from this levy.

Although Justice seems to be effective in its mission, a large proportion of the public still feel strongly that this system should be abolished.

Let's go to the audience.

Yes, the person in the beige cardigan, yes, far left, you are?".

"Nancy Underwood".

"Welcome Nancy. What is it you would like to say, what are your views regarding Justice?".

"I understand that the system is effective, but surely people must see that it is totally and unacceptably intrusive! Not only memory extraction, which alone *must* be viewed as an unacceptable invasion of that person's privacy and their human rights, but also to involve the use of artificial intelligence, as an interface to convert these memories into a vivid reality. I have read about the procedure Cerebral Visual Rendering, CVR, used by the PJO for memory extraction, and this is what I have discovered. Technology which allows for an individual's memories to be analysed, edited, and converted into tangible data files.

In my own words, if I am understanding this correctly, a mind-sweep evokes certain memories, triggered by evidence, specific objects, places, faces and so on, bringing them to the forefront of the mind.

CVR extracts these stimulated memories, and converts them into clear images, filling in any blanks, like a jigsaw puzzle with only a handful of pieces to complete the whole picture.

The final file is then made accessible for the public to view, and vote, if they should so wish!

This, in conjunction with the Justice Sentence, represents a flagrant affront to the principles of humanity and justice, manifesting as an act of sheer cruelty and is unequivocally wrong!

I have heard the final Justice described as 'a hand-made Hell'. Punishment should be left in the hands of God! If people sin, they will face their eternal condemnation when their time in this life comes to an end, and they face their Creator".

(Audience applauds....and jeers)

"Well, thanks Nancy, I was hoping for something a little more original! It's snowflakes like you who will bring this world to its knees!".

"I beg your pardon!".

"You heard me, Nancy!".

"Please, don't shout out at a speaker, wait to be invited. As you've started Sir, please carry on. Could you kindly introduce yourself".

"My name is Mark Shaw, a bloody hardworking father of 4. These bible-bashers, they have no idea, they need to grow a backbone! There's only one way to deal with the scum, that's with a short-sharp-shock or an electric one! The animals who face Justice gave up all rights the moment they committed murder.

For example, Nancy, you're quite happy to send the guilty party, who sexually abused and murdered your innocent child to prison, where they will *live*, be fed hot meals, have a warm place to sleep, even entertainment in most cases and we, the law-abiding, hard-working taxpayers should foot the bill? Do you really believe it's a suitable *punishment* for taking another innocent, human being's life, as you call it, a sin?".

(Audience applauds loudly)

"Would you like to reply to Mark's comments Nancy?".

"Indeed, I would! I believe we should be learning from these situations and showing forgiveness, not hatred. Rehabilitation, counselling, or a prison sentence is required, not the death penalty and certainly not Justice! This makes you no better than them! Compassion needs to be shown in these circumstances!".

"Are you listening to yourself! Compassion! These people are soulless, evil, how can you not see that? So, they go through rehab' and then what? They get released into society to re-offend and back to their cosy prison cell, that's if they're ever caught again and convicted! Get real woman!".

"Personally, *Mister* Shaw, I believe people like you, savages, will turn this world into an uncaring, compassionless, hollow place! I am assuming your short-sharp-shock comment is referring to the Island?

That place should be wiped off the planet! People are suffering terrible deaths for crimes which do not justify such a horrific end!".

"I don't know where you've been living Nancy, cuckoo-land by the sound of it, as this world is already all of those things!

As for the Island, there's not a person who's unaware of the consequences of their actions regarding criminal activities now that the subject is broached within schools. We are all made aware what we will face if convicted. The Island is not only an effective punishment, but also a powerful deterrent, that's why the crime rate has fallen so dramatically!".

(Audience applauds loudly)

"Forgiveness is necessary, not a punishment that is heavy-handed and unjustified. Understanding is what the Human-race is craving, and the reason these people commit such terrible crimes in the first place! Without compassion, we will never become a civilised and loving planet. It is clear from your comments Mister Shaw that the financial benefits of the Justice Organisation are all you are really concerned about!".

"Forgiveness? These people commit their crimes because they're evil, end of story! And yes, I am better off financially with the Organisation in place, and good riddance to the twisted, sick bastards, they deserve their Justice sentence! Seriously Russel, are you hearing this shit?!".

"Thank you both for your extremely strong opinions, but could we please keep the language clean!

Now let's take a breath, as things are becoming quite heated already! Let's go to another speaker, please raise your hands.

The person in the black and red trousers, the second row, yes, you. You are?".

"My name is Mary, Mary Loake. I'd just like to address this to Nancy. What if, like me, you don't have faith, if you don't believe in a God, what then? Should I just *hope* that someone who slaughtered a person I love *may* get what they deserve when they die? How can you expect people without belief to accept this? If someone I loved faced a terrible end, which these animals are more than capable of, I would want to be *sure*, here, and *now*, that they get what they deserve!".

"Here-bloody-here!".

"Mr. Shaw, please!".

"Yes. Well, that's exactly what's wrong with you, no faith! With faith, the PJO would not be required, and if the people committing these offences believed in God, then they would not carry out their crimes, as they would know their punishment would be silently waiting for them, for all of eternity!".

"That's a good point Nancy!".

"And you are?".

"I'm Gerald. Hello everyone!

I agree with most of the points Nancy made. If we were to jump back in time, the justice sentence would not be required, or insect island.

Also, the use of artificial intelligence, even with memories and facts involved, leads me to doubt the accuracy of the evidence presented by the PJO".

"I'm Martin Baxter and what a crock of shite! We aren't living in the Middle Ages now loves!".

(audience laughs...and jeers)

"One speaker at a time, and there's no need for cursing! Please continue Sir".

"It's called evolution, progression, and technology! Just because it didn't exist then, doesn't mean it's wrong for the here-and-now. Things change, improve. It's a process of learning and growing. I'm a hundred and ten per cent behind Justice, it's the only way people will learn and change.

If you deliberately inflict pain onto another human being, and end their life, then you should experience that same suffering and fate, as you said Mr. Shaw, end of story!

This, Nancy is where your compassion nose-dives. Where was theirs, when carrying out their heinous crimes? Nowhere! Some people are just born evil! Justice is our future!".

(Audience applauds loudly)

"Could I add something please Russel?".

"Yes Nancy, please feel free to go on".

"She already has! On-and-on-and-on!".

"Now Mr. Shaw, I won't be asking you again, respect other speakers!"

"Yeah, okay, sorry Russel".

"Go ahead Nancy".

"Mr. Shaw, what happens if eventually, crime *does* become a thing of the past? There will be no cases to vote on, no criminals to be prosecuted, and no way for the PJO to raise necessary funding to pay for ongoing sentences! Who will foot the bill then? *Us*, that is who!".

"Well *Nance*, I'm sure this has already been considered and I doubt your shallow little mind is the first to raise this question!

I have total confidence in the PJO and believe they will introduce something which will raise the necessary funding. They're slightly more intelligent than you, which to be frank, wouldn't be too difficult, would it!".

"Mr. Shaw that's enough! There's no need to become personal, we're all entitled to our own opinion! I think it's time to take a quick break.

Thank you all for your comments, we'll be back shortly".

14

Jessie suddenly woke, the bay quiet and empty, with just the glow of the television screen lighting the darkness. She pulled up her covers and grabbed the visor.

'Load, Alfie Docherty, Buried Alive, Play'.

Narrator

"Permission has been granted by Alfie's family for public viewing. These heartbreaking memories prove that Sutton is evil beyond belief and deserves no mercy.

Alfie, a young lad of only 12-years of age, was returning home from an amusement arcade, when Sutton kidnapped the youngster, taking him to his underground bunker at Marshdown woods...."

The bay doors opened and once again, much to Jessie's annoyance, Nurse Andrews entered with a tray of drinks.

"Come on now Jessie, off with the VIV, it's lights out in 15 minutes", ordered the nurse.

Jessie yanked off the visor and scowled at her.

"What are you watching, nothing to give you bad dreams I should hope?".

"No, of course not! I'm not thirsty, is it okay if I continue on here?", asked Jessie desperately.

"No, it's lights out!", barked the nurse.

Jessie glared, obviously annoyed.

"I'll be back early in the morning with your medication. Lights out soon, goodnight", she said, as she set down the tray onto Jessie's bedside table.

"I still haven't seen Mr. Northern, I need to talk to him, have you any idea when he'll see me?".

"Sometime tomorrow, you're not the only patient he has you know!", barked the nurse.

"Fine!", snapped Jessie.

Jessie lay awake after lights out. She was feeling frustrated, as she looked at the visor on Anna's bedside table, where Nurse Andrews had deliberately placed it.

Eventually she drifted off to sleep.

15

"That's a bright and cheerful window scene to be waking up to girls, how are you all feeling this fine morning", smiled Mr. Northern, as he passed Anna and Holly, both with their visors on, sat on their beds.

"I'm good thank you *Mr. Northern*", giggled Holly, as Anna raised her crutch and waved.

"Oh. Jessie. Well. Just look at you! Have you done something different with your hair!?".

Jessie could hear the girls sniggering and once again, began to feel self-conscious.

"Why do you keep laughing at me all the time, you're making me feel paranoid. I'm getting really sick of it now!", she growled angrily.

"We've already told you, we never laugh at you, it's all in your head!", Anna hollered back.

"I heard you!".

"Ah, hun, why would we do that, we're all besties, aren't we?", smirked Holly.

"Jessie calm down! No one was making fun of you.

It isn't unusual for someone with a brain injury to feel insecure and experience feelings of paranoia, it's quite common. If it continues, please let me know, as there's an abundance of medication which could help", Mr. Northern told her.

"Yes, maybe I do need something!", agreed a worried Jessie.

"Ok, I'll make an appointment for you as soon as possible for an assessment, and we'll get things moving", he assured her, then turned his attention to Anna and Holly.

"Girls, why don't you take some time out, you must need a break by now, come with me", he said, gesturing them with his hand to follow him, as he headed towards the door.

"Five more minutes and we're done", Anna told him, and Holly nodded.

"Astounding!", he smiled, and left the bay.

"Could you pass me the VIV Anna, if you've finished with it?" asked Jessie.

"Surely you aren't going in for more?", snapped Anna, throwing her a disapproving stare. "Don't forget I'm paying for all these visits!", she reminded Jessie angrily.

"I'm only watching the free documentaries on how Justice started", Jessie continued lying. "I'm looking forward to watching Garth Sutton on the reality TV program soon though!", she added excitedly.

"Well, you've already missed the first one!", smirked Anna.

"When was that on, I've not heard anything about it!", fumed Jessie, annoyed that no one had bothered to tell her when it was being aired.

"Ah well, what a shame you missed it, but we'll make sure you catch up!", grinned Holly.

"Well thanks a bunch for letting me know!", raged Jessie, as the girls just turned their backs and headed towards the door.

"Come on Anna, let's go and have a wander around. Are you not coming, hun? Oops, sorry, I forgot, you're chained to your bed", laughed Holly, as they headed out the door, leaving Jessie seething.

16

<u>The People's Justice Organisation</u>
<u>Signs Department</u>

"Morning Geoff, did you have a good day off?", asked Joe, as he entered through sliding glass doors into the Signs Office.

"Yeah, it was a good one mate, I ended up playing golf for most of it, avoiding the Mrs. and a visit from the mother-in-law", he laughed.

"Golf! I'd rather watch paint dry", smiled Joe. "I don't have the mum-in-law problem either, but I'm still suffering from one too many drinks I had last night", he yawned, as he rubbed his hands over his unshaven face, his short, fair hair uncombed and messy.

"So, Geoff, what's on the agenda for today, I guess we'll be getting really busy soon, now that the Sutton murders are available for viewing?".

"Without a doubt. We'd better get ready for some overtime", he warned, peering at Joe over his gold-rimmed glasses.

"We've got the new recruit coming in today, so we have to show her the ropes. We're going to need her help, as countless people are being flagged in the Vault already", Geoff reminded him.

"You're kidding, is that today? I'm not sure my heads up to it", complained Joe.

"Yup, I'm afraid so. Don't worry, I'll sort her out if you're still hung-over", laughed Geoff.

"Cheers mate, I appreciate it. I'll get a black coffee before she arrives; would you like one?".

"No thanks, I've not long had one", said Geoff, as Joe disappeared out the door.

Geoff looked at the computer screen in front of him and touched the icon, *flagged*. A long list of people's names loaded.

"And here it starts", he said to himself, as the office doors whooshed open, and he spun around in his seat, as the signs manager and a tall, attractive brunette entered the room.

"Good morning Geoff, this is Jackie Mason. Just to confirm she's already signed the Organisation's Official Secrets Act and has the cleansing nanobug implant, so, it's all systems go. Get her up to speed as soon as possible please".

"Hello Jackie, I'm Geoff Baker, nice to meet you", he said, as he stood and offered her his hand, which she shook firmly.

"Nice to meet you too", she smiled.

"Thanks Geoff. Once you're finished here if you could report back to my office please Jackie, we have more paperwork to look through".

"Yes, of course", she nodded, as the manager left.

Joe suddenly stumbled through the doors, spilling his coffee all over the floor, oblivious of Jackie standing on the far side of the room.

"Ah, crap!", he shouted, as he tried to wipe off the coffee stain from his trousers.

Geoff cleared his throat, trying to get Joe's attention, and Jackie covered her mouth with her hand, trying to hide her amusement.

"Joe, this is Jackie. Jackie, Joe. She's here for her induction", Geoff introduced them.

"Oh. Very nice! To meet you I mean", grinned Joe, as he walked over.

"Thanks, and you", she smiled.

"Well, I've checked the signs log and they're coming in thick and fast already, so the sooner we get you up to speed Jackie the better. It can be a bit mundane sometimes, but there's a quiet satisfaction knowing that you could be saving lives", explained Geoff.

"Great, let's get on with it then, I'll take it from here", said Joe, who was now eagerly sat at his workstation.

He patted the chair next to his, signalling to Jackie, who walked over and sat down.

Geoff rolled his eyes and sat at another workstation, knowing Joe's sudden eagerness shown he had ulterior motives.

"It's quite straightforward really", Joe began to explain.

"This is the signs screen. It displays a list of names and locations of anyone who's visiting the Vault using their VIV. So, see, right now there's over 93,000 people watching files in our designated area, that's quite low, but it's early hours.

The pads in their visor, which are cushioned against their temples, record any thoughts and emotions they're having, which are relayed back to the Organisation's computers. Anyone having unsavoury ideas or feelings, for example, if they're getting aroused watching a murder file, or they're viewing a terrorist attack and thinking of a plot themselves, then they're flagged and their details appear in this drop-down file here, see?".

He tapped the screen to demonstrate, and a long list of names with locations began to scroll down.

"These are the ones we're interested in. Each person here has been flagged, so we need to monitor them. If they're deemed to be high risk, then a nanobug implant will be considered. This is all without their knowledge. This information is highly confidential, that's why you've already signed the O.S.A. and had your implant.

If you begin to think about disclosing any of these details, certain thoughts will trigger memory cleansing, and erase all information associated with the bugs.

If any details regarding the nanobugs were ever to become public knowledge, it would be the end of the Organisation. I'm sure you're already aware of this".

"Yes, I understand. I don't like the idea of a bug nested in my brain though, it makes me feel queasy", laughed Jackie.

Joe grinned.

"The nanobugs are microscopic and resemble a robotic scarab. They're programmed to seek out their target, entering through their nasal passage. They bore their way through the cerebral cortex and attach themselves to the frontal lobes, activating the implant, sending their host's thoughts here to the PJO. There have never been any adverse effects. Anyone who has been flagged will be monitored and our main objective is to ensure everything is running smoothly.

The Organisation's 'A-Eye' software takes care of most of the legwork, remotely accessing devices, viewing browsing history, current and past employment, bank account information, purchases, telephone calls, criminal record background checks and so on. If we decide that an implant is the best option, then a bug would be sent out to its target.

The Organisation are currently developing a neuro-visual recorder, capturing everything which the host sees.

I imagine it would be much like a data stream, which could be saved as a video file, and stored here at the PJO. Maybe in 50-years-or-so that may be a reality".

"I think the world would instantaneously combust if society ever found out", joked Jackie.

"You could be right there!", agreed Geoff. "What made you want to come and work in the Signs Department?".

"I'm here because I care. I've been working within the Organisation for over 9 years. My younger brother was murdered, and his killer has yet to be caught. It's been over 6 years now and I want to make a difference. I'm praying that I may even get lucky and come across the thoughts of his killer".

"You would need more than luck I'm afraid Jackie. There's over two and a half billion people who own a VIV, and only four hundred signs departments throughout the world, even though it's expanding fast, the chances of you finding his killer are extremely remote. I'm very sorry to hear about your brother and for your loss", said Geoff.

"Thank you. Even though it's been years it doesn't get any easier. I still miss him terribly and the thought of his killer still free is so upsetting and frustrating, that's the main reason I decided to transfer", she explained sadly.

"That must be very hard to deal with", sympathised Joe.

Jackie nodded. "So, has there been any feedback about Sutton, do you think he would have been rehabilitated given the opportunity?".

"No way! My mate Roger, in the Senses Department, told me it's all been negative readings. Sutton's thoughts reveal there's been no change. He's still an evil son of a bitch, thinking about what he'd like to do to others if he had the chance. He never deserved rehab' as far as I'm concerned, not after what he did!", ranted Geoff.

"Did you watch the first reality program and hear some of his thoughts?", asked Joe.

"Yes, I watched a few minutes, but if I'm honest I couldn't stomach any more, it's just too gory, it makes me feel ill. I've already cast my vote and I'll tune in to see him face the Final Justice tomorrow, although for most of the time I'll probably have it on mute with my eyes closed", she laughed.

"Yeah, I know what you mean! Even though they should suffer, it's still difficult to watch", agreed Joe.

"Well, I won't be looking away, I want to see his face, it's nothing he doesn't deserve!", growled Geoff angrily.

"We're already inundated with flags, it's always the way when it's a serial killer", said Joe.

"Well, I'm raring to go, where do I start?", asked Jackie.

17

Jessie had just finished her lunch and immediately grabbed the visor, hiding beneath her bedding, feeling Anna had been keeping tabs on her.

'Load, Rose Foster, Play'.

Narrator

"5-year-old Rose was abducted from her bed in 2073, as her parents slept.

The little girl was taken by Sutton to his bunker in Marshdown woods, where he repeatedly beat, sexually assaulted, and tortured the helpless child for an unimaginable 9 days.

Her father, Richard Foster, released a heartbreaking written statement on national television, begging,

'We just want our little girl back. She is our world, our baby, the heart of our family'.

Sutton's memories show him listening to the appeals, laughing aloud, and declaring, 'you shall get your wish'.

12 days later a package was found in a public park labelled, 'To Mummy & Daddy', which was later confirmed to contain the heart of the missing child.

The world was left speechless. An evil beyond belief".

Jessie scanned through the available files.

'Load, Rose Foster's remains through Sutton's own eyes'.

"Permission has been granted by Mr. and Mrs. Foster for public viewing of this extremely upsetting and disturbing memory".

'View'.

Jessie travelled through the misty tunnel and impatiently waited for the picture to clear.

She was there, walking through a thick, wooded area. She could see the figure of a tiny body being carried before her, as if she were holding it in her own arms.

Wrapped in a black refuse bag, a child's small, limp arms were visible, hanging lifelessly.

Sutton, with a spade held under his arm stopped, cocked his elbow, letting the spade drop from his grip.

He threw his arms forwards into the air, holding onto the plastic, and a tiny body spiralled down onto the leaf-covered floor.

Jessie paused the memory, as Sutton stared at the remains of little Rose, and she stared through his eyes, at what was almost unrecognisable as a human being.

He grabbed the spade and began to dig a deep hole, and Jessie skipped the memories forward for several minutes.

Sutton coldly kicked Rose's tiny body into the grave, then began shovelling the dirt on top of her, as the images began to fade.

Narrator

"After viewing Sutton's memories, the authorities discovered Rose Foster's remains, and her parents were finally able to lay their young daughter to rest".

Once again, much to her annoyance, Jessie was interrupted by Nurse Andrews and quickly removed the visor.

She started to think that the nurse was deliberately trying to annoy her!

She picked up a computer notepad and tried to look interested in a dull article about gardening, eagerly waiting for her to leave.

"Holly, Holly, your parents are here to collect you, are you ready?", shouted Nurse Andrews, as she walked over and picked up a large case, sitting on the floor at the front of the bay, and placed it onto an auto-trolley.

"Yes, I'm raring to go!", squealed Holly.

"Come on, let's get you home sweetheart, it's all over now", smiled Nurse Andrews kindly.

"Bye then *hun!*", shouted Holly as she headed towards the door.

"Yeah, whatever", sulked Jessie, the jealousy biting at her.

18

Heather's mum helped her into the rear of the car and walked round to the boot, struggling as she put the heavy case inside.

"Can you manage Jean?", shouted her husband from the driver's seat.

"Yes Pete, I've got it!", she called.

"Are you ok love?", he asked, as he looked at his daughter through the rear-view mirror.

Heather could only see her dad's framed, deep-green eyes, but the creases beneath his grey, thinning hair indicated a concerned smile.

"I'm alright dad, I just can't wait to get home, have a hot bath and some rest", she sighed.

As Jean slammed the boot shut, Heather let out a shrill scream and threw herself into the footwell, trembling with fear.

Jean rushed and held her gently, as she sobbed uncontrollably into her mother's chest.

"My baby girl, my brave, brave girl. It's over now. We're so proud of you!", sobbed Jean.

Pete paused and waited for his wife to lower herself into the backseat.

Heather took hold of her mother's long hair and twisted the soft, sandy curls around her fingers, as she had often done as a child, and began to feel safe and comforted.

"Let's get you home. I'll cook you something special love, whatever you fancy", smiled Pete.

Heather sniffled.

"Thanks, but I think I'd rather mum cook!", she tried to joke.

"Oh, charming, cheeky! Is there anything you'd like to pick up on our way home?", he asked, with intermittent glances at Heather, as he quickly made his way from the carpark to join the long, winding country road, a direct path to their home.

"Pete, watch the road!", ordered Jean.

"Yes love", he tutted, as Heather saw him roll his eyes.

"Did you see Abbie before she left Shorelands?", asked Jean.

"Yes, Abbie and I spent most of our time together. I'll see her next at the counselling sessions", said Heather.

"Everything will feel different after this weekend, I promise you, things will get easier, and once you've completed your reconstructive surgery, we can work at regaining some of your confidence", enthused Jean.

Heather stared out of the window, as the countryside flashed past, its beauty now lost to her, replaced with a deep feeling of dread and fear – the repulsiveness she felt for herself was somehow magnified by it.

They reached their home, a quaint cottage situated at the end of a pretty-pebbled drive, once picturesque to Heather, but now lost inside her too. She could not bear to see attractiveness or beauty in anything anymore, her grotesque appearance turned her stomach. She prayed that her upcoming surgery and counselling would help.

"Come on then love, let's get you inside", fussed Pete, as he held open the front door.

As soon as Heather entered, she knew her mum had been busy preparing for her arrival home. The smell of boiled apples, bread, coffee and what she guessed was a chicken-stew, all merged into a sickening stench.

"Mmm, something smells good", said Pete, licking his lips.

"I've prepared chicken coq-au-vin", smiled Jean, as she helped Heather ease herself into a chair at their rustic wooden table – an autumn scene cushion offered little comfort to her pain.

"I was going to cook!", complained Pete, as he walked over to a large slow cooker, removed the lid, and an escaping steam cloud misted his glasses.

"Yes, so I see", he laughed, looking to Heather, but she was in no mood for joking.

"I'm not hungry at the moment, I think I'll go take a bath and try to get some sleep", she yawned.

"Are you tired already, it's early yet?", said Jean, looking concerned.

"I haven't slept well recently", winced Heather, as she tentatively raised herself from the chair.

"I'll help you upstairs", said Jean, as she walked towards her daughter.

"It's ok mum, I need to start managing for myself".

"But it's no trouble sweetheart, I'll..."

"Stop fussing, I'll be fine, I'm only going for a soak!", snapped Heather.

"Yes. Yes, ok. I'm sorry", apologised Jean, who looked sadly towards Pete – his lips pursed together, as he gave a sorrowful smile, as he watched his daughter slowly, and desperately struggle up the stairs.

Heather began to run the bath and looked around the small, pretty, peach tiled bathroom, which her mum had obviously prepared for her.

Freshly picked, deep-burgundy dahlias, once Heather's favourite, sat on the window ledge in a white vase. She pulled on the cord of the blind, closing it fully to hide them from her sight.

She gathered up the candles, which had been carefully and lovingly placed around the edges of the freestanding porcelain bath and dropped them into a wicker basket next to the locked door.

A full-length mirror in the corner reflected the agony of her past.

Her skin stretched and tightened over her scars and a yelp of pain left her, as she draped a heavy, white bath-towel over the wooden frame.

Pain seared through her, as she lowered herself into the tepid water, hiding her scarred body beneath a thick layer of bubbles floating on the surface.

Her exhausted eyes began to close almost instantly, as she continued to fight the overpowering, desperate need for sleep.

***

Heather came around to the pitch of darkness, the stench, so over-powering, she could taste it.

She gasped, gulping in putrid air, which burnt through her lungs like moulten metal.

She clamped her hand over her mouth, as she gagged and retched, unable to hold back the acidic bile, which projected between her mutilated, bloodstained fingers.

Something ice-cold and wet pressed against her cheek – she didn't want to know what it was, but she knew... *she knew.*

"Please dear God, please be there", a faint, desperate voice sobbed, only just audible – distorted by pain and muffled by the thin wood of a coffin.

"I'm here Abbie! I hear you!", screamed Heather.

Their uncontrollable joy at hearing each other's voices was smothered beneath their sobs... then panic!

"No! Shush, shush, he'll hear us, we must whisper!", cried Heather.

"There's something in here with me, it stinks!", screeched Abbie, as Heather felt she was suffocating, an unbearable, claustrophobic feeling taking hold of her.

"I can too, but we have to keep quiet, or he'll know we're awake!", she shouted, but the revving of the engine masked her pleas.

Heather desperately tried to move, to free herself, but began to cough and choke. She tilted her head and spat – the bitter bile now replaced with the sharp, metallic taste of blood.

"Oh Jesus, it's his remains! Oh, sweet Jesus, he's put Jason in here with me!", wailed Abbie, as she thrashed and screamed, "Let me out, get me out!".

"You must calm down! Calm down! He will hear you!", begged Heather.

Abbie suddenly silenced. "Where do you think he's taking us? Is he going to bury us, or burn us, where is he going, why now, what if...!".

"I don't know!", yelled Heather.

"Someone, anyone, please help us!", sobbed Abbie.

The screech of the tyres stopped their cries instantly, as the coffins were thrown violently from their restraints. They skidded forward and smashed into the front panel, behind the driver's seat of the large transit van.

"What the hell was that!", screamed Abbie.

"Quiet. I think he's crashed", said Heather, her eyes trying to focus, adjusting to a bright light shining through a small split in the wood. "I think I can push this, wait, wait!", she yelled; her teeth clenched, as she rammed her shoulder into the splintered wood.

"It's going, it's going", she wailed, as she thrust her way through the side of the coffin, unable to contain her piercing cries.

She was free!

She scrambled to her feet and frantically looked around, trying to find something to help release Abbie.

She rummaged through a mountain of bulging garbage bags, tearing at the plastic, and a severed hand, writhing with maggots fell to the floor.

She covered her mouth with her arm; the stench of rotting flesh burning, like acid in her lungs.

"We have to get out of here right now!", she shrieked.

"Are you out. Oh my God, get me out, please, please, don't leave me!", begged Abbie, her banging now at its most frantic.

"I won't leave you, I swear!", promised Heather, as she tried to focus, spotting a spade lying next to her feet.

Her bloody fingers grasped the handle, her severed skin split open by its weight, but she pushed back the pain, and thrust the rusted metal under the loosened coffin lid. A scream tore through her, as she levered the spade upward, pushing it further under the lid, until finally, it came free.

She dragged the coffin lid off and reeled back, her hand jumped to her mouth, as she tried to force back the vomit rising in her throat. The gruesomeness of Abbie's deformed, mutilated face wrenched her gut.

She grabbed Abbie's arm, trying to ease her up, as they wailed in agony.

"What should we do? Grab something, anything!", Abbie screamed. "If he comes in the back, hit the mother fucker hard!".

Heather grabbed the spade and headed towards the double doors at the back of the van.

"What have you got?", whispered Abbie.

"A spade".

"That's good, that's great! If he opens that door don't just swing at him, you make sure you jab it straight at his throat as hard as you can! Chop his fuckin' head off!", ordered Abbie.

"Don't you worry, I will!", stamped Heather, a sudden bravery taking hold of her.

"Can you see, can you walk?", she winced at the sight of Abbie's severed flesh, hanging from the bone of her knee, her eye socket clotted with ebony-blood.

"I have some vision in my right eye, but I sure as fuck can get the hell out of here, that I know!", and Heather knew she meant it.

Heather took hold of the handle and paused.

"What if it's locked? You know how careful he is, he's not stupid!", she panicked, her hands shaking wildly.

"Try it! If it's locked, we'll find another way. He'll have to come and check on us soon, then that will be our chance. Go on, pull it. Now!", screamed Abbie.

Heather pulled gently on the handle… nothing.

"Pull it harder!", screeched Abbie.

"It's no use, it's locked!".

"Yank it, for fuck's sake, go on!".

Heather pulled hard on the handle, and the door suddenly clicked and slowly swung open.

"Holy crap, I told you! Take your time now", whispered Abbie.

Heather peered out into the dusky countryside. Trees, fields, and hedgerows stretched out as far as she could see, a long, winding, road ahead of her.

"What should we do, do we go now, I can't walk, he'll catch us, we don't stand a chance!", panicked Abbie.

"We must try. Here, take this!", said Heather and handed Abbie a sheet of blue plastic, and wrapped her naked body in another – sweat, blood and weeping flesh held it in place.

"I'm going to see where he is", she told Abbie bravely.

"Are you fuckin' crazy! He'll see you, then we're both dead!", screamed Abbie.

"I'm going. I'll be back for you, I swear!".

"No! No! Please, I beg you, don't go! He'll get you, and then he'll be back for me!", sobbed Abbie.

"I have to!", said Heather, clutching the spade firmly.

She stood for several seconds, thrusting her weapon forward, trying to get a feel for it, her skin burning as the cold air hit her.

She stumbled from the van, as Abbie's sobs rang in her ears.

The road was desolate, and a moonlight haze was masked behind angry clouds.

Heather crept towards the front door of the van, which had hit a tree and was a tangle of metal. She could see a large, dead deer beneath the chassis; its intestines splayed across the floor. She cringed and gagged, as her feet squelched and sank into the grass, which was soaked in the animal's blood and guts.

She shook violently, as she peered through the window.

She reeled back, stumbled, and fell into a bush, at the shock of seeing her captor.

She scrambled to her feet, grappling for the spade.

She didn't want to look, she was petrified, but knew she must, she had to remember him, remember the details of the man who had done this to them.

The monster was unconscious, slumped over the steering wheel, his head pumping blood from a deep wound.

Heather took a step closer and peered through the broken window, her heart pounding in her ears like a drum, oblivious of the shattered glass which crunched beneath her bare feet, her body numb with fear.

Grasped in his hand, his fingernails rife with filth and blood, was a small, white teddy bear.

Heather knew she *must* save it.

She crept silently closer and leant into the window, the jagged glass scraped against her chest. Each breath she held, as she carefully, gently, and slowly began to prise the bear from his tight grip.

Suddenly his hollow, deadeyes sprang open and locked onto hers.

Heather froze.

His pale, gaunt face contorted in anger, as he lunged and clawed at her arm, growling like a wild animal.

She threw herself backwards, his grip slick with his blood, and she slipped away, the bear scrunched tightly inside her hand.

She instantly pushed herself to her feet, and armed herself with the spade, as she stared back into the van.

The monster had collapsed, motionless.

Heather, unsure whether he was alive or dead, released a gut-wrenching, blood curdling scream.

'They had to go. They had to go now!', she yelled inside her head.

"Heather, are you alright, you've been an awfully long time?", shouted Jean.

Heather gasped and pushed herself from the freezing water. She jumped from the bath in one quick movement, as pain surged through every nerve of her body.

She unlocked the door and threw herself into her mother's arms.

"Oh, my poor baby. It's ok, you're safe, shush now, shush. It won't be long, it will all be wiped away soon", sobbed Jean.

19

"Nice to see you and Anna back Holly", laughed Jessie, with obvious delight and a sarcastic tone, as she began to hunt around her bedside table for the visor, throwing magazines around frantically.

"Anna! Anna! Have you seen the VIV?", she shouted in panic.

"I have it, if that's ok with you!", scowled Anna.

"Oh, that's a relief", calmed Jessie.

"I never did manage to find the reality TV program, but I'm looking forward to watching the final", grinned Jessie.

"Well, it's almost time. Sutton's Final Justice is tonight", Holly told her.

"What's the show about though?", asked Jessie.

Holly sighed.

"We've told you already. It's Sutton receiving his punishment.

It's broadcast all over the world, live, and only available on the VIV. It takes place in front of the families of the victims and any survivors", she explained.

"I can't wait", laughed Jessie.

"No, neither can we", said Holly, as all three girls laughed.

"It's a shame you won't have a VIV to watch it on though", smirked Anna.

"What! No! What do you mean?", hollered Jessie.

"Obviously I'll be using mine", smirked Anna.

"You have got to be fuckin' kidding me! I tell you what, you're lucky I can't get out of this bed, because I'd rip your other fuckin' eye out, you ugly, deformed bitch! I'd ram that visor right down your fuckin' throat!", raged Jessie.

Jessie had buried herself beneath her bedding, boiling inside with anger and rage.

She was relieved when she heard Mr. Northern enter the bay.

"Mr. Northern, Mr. Northern, I need to talk to you right now!".

"Yes, of course Jessie, I've already booked us a consultation room. Let's get you unhooked, and I'll take you there myself", he smiled. "Nurse Andrews will be joining us to offer you some support. Come on now, into the chair", he said, as he helped Jessie from the bed.

"*Into the chair!* I bet you'll be wishing that's where you *were* going!*", laughed Anna.

"Oh, good one!", laughed Holly.

"What's that supposed to mean!", growled Jessie.

"What do you mean?", Mr. Northern asked.

"That ugly bitches comment just then!", fumed Jessie.

"Jessie, calm down, no one has said anything. Come now, let's get you to the consultation room", he said, and instructed the self-nav' wheelchair out of the bay.

"Bye *Jess*, I hope it's nothing too serious *hun*", laughed Holly, as Anna howled in hysterics, as Jessie was wheeled away.

Mr. Northern followed her down a long corridor and into the only room on the left, as the girl's laughter slowly faded.

Nurse Andrews was already seated on the far side of a large conference table, and Mr. Northern joined the nurse, as Jessie sat alone, desperately wondering what they were about to tell her.

"I'm afraid we have some bad news for you. Your scans have been checked and it appears there's a tiny bone fragment still lodged in your brain. Although at this time, it isn't causing any problems, your body may start rejecting it and this could have some serious implications", explained Mr. Northern.

"How could you have missed that. What's going to happen?", yelled Jessie.

"We've arranged for you to undergo emergency surgery; we need to remove it as soon as possible", he said.

"I'm not prepared!".

"Come now Jessie, be brave. You're strong and healthy and you'll be in the hands of one of the country's top brain surgeons, won't you? You know you can trust him", smiled Nurse Andrews.

"It's taken me months to get over my last surgery, I just want to get out of here. I feel like an alien trapped inside this body!", stormed Jessie.

"Think of Anna and Holly and how they've suffered. They've undergone endless operations and counselling and still have so far to go!", snapped Mr. Northern.

"I couldn't care less about what those bitches have suffered!", raged Jessie.

"Don't you feel anything for the girls, no compassion or sorrow for what they've endured?", asked the nurse.

"No, nothing. I honestly couldn't give a shit, it serves the scheming bitches right", she growled coldly.

"This must be done. Room 2 please nurse and prep her for surgery", said Mr. Northern.

"You have to be joking, what right now?", yelled Jessie.

"Yes, right now, it's time", grinned Mr. Northern, as he rubbed his hands together vigorously.

20

"Come on Abbie, this way, we've a surprise for you!", said Mac, hardly able to contain his excitement, as he rushed ahead along the corridor of the clinic Confidence Regained.

Sally squeezed Abbie's hand, as they hurried past promotional, cinematic advertisements on each of the clinic walls, the presentations running unsynchronised and almost impossible to decipher.

"Where are we going Sally, I'm not booked in for another counselling session yet?", Abbie asked her sister curiously.

"You'll see", she smiled. "Abbie's going to love this, isn't she dad", Sally glowed, looking towards Mac, who nodded.

"Ah, there! Sarah Clement, Cosmetic Consultant, this is the lady", he said, pointing to a gold nameplate on a door.

"Recon' Surgery, but I've already started", said Abbie, totally baffled.

Sally grinned, as Mac knocked firmly on the door.

"Please come in!", a woman's voice called.

"Abbie!", shouted Heather and tentatively wrapped her in a hug.

"Oh, Heather it's great to see you!", smiled Abbie, as she gave her a gentle squeeze. "What's going on, do you know?".

Heather shrugged and looked as equally puzzled.

"Mac, Sally, I believe you already know Pete and Jean Marlow, Heather's parents", smiled the doctor.

"We do indeed. Lovely to see you both", said Mac, and shook their hands in turn.

"It's really good to see you all, and on such an exciting occasion too!", smiled Pete.

"Oh, please, what occasion?", asked Abbie impatiently.

"Yes, come on, what's going on?", asked Heather.

"Please, if you could all take a seat, we don't want to keep the girls in suspense any longer", laughed the doctor.

"Thank you, Doctor Clement", said Jean.

"Please, call me Sarah. Abbie, Heather, welcome", she smiled.

"Your parents have brought you here today to introduce you to a new product, which will be marketed by the clinic within the next couple of weeks. We'd like to give you the opportunity to try it out before its official release by Confidence Regained.

It's simply called a VIB, which represents its full title, the Visage Image Band.

It's not a product which will be available to the public, it will be considered exclusively for our clients, and we felt that it could benefit you both immensely.

It's a temporary fix whilst you await your bio-printed-artificial body parts and transplants", explained the doctor.

There are some terms of use to be considered, but if you're interested, I have a VIB for each of you to try".

"Yes please", nodded Abbie.

"But what does the band actually do?", asked Heather.

"It's going to give you your faces back", smiled the doctor, as she handed them each a clear, pliable band.

"It's so light and floppy, I can't imagine what you would do with it", laughed Heather, as she flapped it around in the air.

"It's like a thin, wobbly jelly", laughed Abbie.

"If you look at it closely, on one side you will see a maze of circuitry and a downward arrow, can you see it?", asked the doctor.

"Oh yes, found it", said Abbie, as Heather was still searching.

"You've got your finger over it!", laughed Abbie.

"Oh. Yup, got it!", grinned Heather.

"If you place the band at the top of your head, as central as you can, with the arrow pointing to the floor, it will adhere to your skin", said the doctor.

Heather removed her mask and adjusted her headscarf.

"Done", said Abbie.

"It's stuck fast", said Heather.

"Ok girls. The bands are pre-programmed with your images, using photographs your family provided, and your bone structures have been analysed and saved, so they're ready to go.

I've entered your personal information into this control pad, it's a small touchscreen. Here", she said, handing them both a small, transparent rectangle. "It's ready for you to enter your identification. Hold the screen at arms-length from your face, and a large, red cross should appear. Abbie, this should make it easier for you to grip", she said, and clipped the device onto a plastic rod with a large handle. "If you could line the cross up between your eyes, the screen will return to clear once your face scan is complete", the doctor continued to explain.

"Oh, it's done!" said Heather.

"Mine too, that was quick!", said Abbie.

"Now girls, tap the screen and repeat, the same process, but just before you do that, if you could come to the back of the room, then you can see the results".

They all stood and made their way to the rear wall, where the doctor uncovered a large mirror.

"If you wouldn't mind stepping back please, just the girls up front", she asked the others.

"Of course,", said Mac, who out-stretched his arms and shuffled everyone backwards.

"Would you like to go one at a time, or together?", asked the doctor.

"Same time!", agreed the girls.

"Ready?", Abbie looked to Heather, as they held out their screens.

"After three. 3-2-1, go…!".

"Oh my God!... Look… look, oh I can't believe it. Look dad, it's me! Sally, Heather, look!", squealed Abbie.

Heather stood silently staring.

"Are you alright baby", asked Jean, who was already in tears and quickly made her way over, closely followed by Pete.

"Look, mum, dad! It's how I was, how I used to look, before he…before… It's me!", sobbed Heather, as Jean gently wrapped her arms around her.

"It's, it's just, unbelievable!", wept Heather.

"Look at my eyes!", cried Abbie.

Doctor Clement handed out tissues to everyone, keeping the box for herself.

"I can run an information video now if you'd like me to girls", the doctor sniffled.

"No, no, it's ok, I'm sold!", laughed an ecstatic Heather.

"Me too. Oh wow, it's simply amazing. Look, Heather, we're back!", beamed Abbie.

"I do need to run through the terms of use", the doctor interrupted, as both girls continued staring at their reflections, giggling, and touching their faces.

"Just stay where you are girls, it will only take a moment, a couple of signatures and they're yours.

The VIB must only be used as pre-programmed by Confidence Regained. Under no circumstances should you ever try to re-program the band with any other images. This is against the New World Law and will result in prosecution, your band being confiscated and all contact with the company terminated.

Anyone attempting to use a VIB for any purpose, other than its cosmetic intentions, will be prosecuted to the full.

A couple of *I agree to* boxes to check, and a quick signature and we're all done!".

"Oh, thank you. Thank you so much Sarah, they're mind-blowing!", said Abbie.

"Yes, thank you, I honestly cannot say that enough!", beamed Heather.

"You are both so very welcome", smiled the doctor.

"Thank you Sarah. You have no idea what this means to the girls", said Jean, firmly shaking her hand.

"It's my pleasure. If you have any concerns at all, please contact me, I'm so happy for them", she said sincerely.

"So, we're all happy!", shouted Pete, as Jean and Sally blew their noses.

"Come on then, let's get home after we stop off for pizza, we don't have long before it's showtime!", buzzed Mac.

21

The People's Justice Arena

"Welcome to the Final Justice!", shouted the host, as dramatic music began to fade.

"We're here tonight, live, from the People's Justice arena!".

The audience erupted in rapturous applause.

"Before we get going, I'd like to say a special welcome to each of the family members and of course, the two surviving victims, who, I would like to add, are the most courageous young women I've ever had the pleasure of meeting!".

The crowd exploded and jumped to their feet in a standing ovation, as the girls waved from their front row seats.

The host waited several minutes for the applause to die down before continuing.

"Now let's introduce you all to our star guest!", he shouted.

Dramatic music began, and the stage lights dimmed, as Sutton, lying on a stretcher, was wheeled into the arena by two men wearing long, white coats. He was placed in the centre of the stage and his shroud removed.

They pushed a bar down on the frame beneath the weighted stretcher and it pivoted forward, until almost vertical. They clicked the bar into place, plugged in a large cable and left the stage.

Sutton's head was slumped forward. He had large, brown pads stuck to each temple and leather restraining straps around his neck, arms, and waist, which suspended him upright, in a standing position.

"Awww, he's still sleeping, should we give him a little nudge?", asked the host, as he held the microphone towards the crowd.

A resounding cheer of "Yes!" echoed, as the deafening applause continued.

The arena was full to its 1500-seat capacity. The audience members were seated behind a clear, bullet-proof screen, with only the surviving victims and the victims' families sitting in front of the safety guard.

The walls of the arena were cinematic screens, the broadcast visible from every angle.

"Work your magic guys", shouted the host, as he gave a thumbs-up towards a large, glass room situated on the second level of the arena.

The lights faded to darkness, and a spotlight illuminated an unconscious Sutton.

"Welcome back!", shouted the host, as Sutton slowly began to come around, his eyes trying to adjust and focus on his surroundings.

Jessie squinted, disorientated, and confused, as the bright ward lights dazzled her eyes.

"Where am I... who are you? You look familiar", she questioned.

"One thing at a time. Just call me Russel. Your operation went well, you'll soon be back to your old self", he told her.

"Oh, thank God! I cannot begin to tell you how relieved I am", sighed Jessie. "I would like to speak to Mr. Northern now".

Russel began to laugh.

"Well, let's get Mr. Northern in here shall we, after all, he *is* the *expert brain surgeon,* isn't he! Come on in here Sir, you can have a quick chat about how the amputation went", said Russel, gesturing with his hand.

"Amputation? I underwent brain surgery", Jessie corrected him, as Mr. Northern entered.

"Did it go well Mr. Northern, I thought I'd be remembering things by now, but I don't feel any different?", Jessie questioned him.

"Are you feeling any pain, are you nice and comfortable?", asked Mr. Northern.

"No pain. I'm still numb, but I feel fine", Jessie assured him.

"Don't you worry, any time now that's all going to change, we're all looking forward to it immensely", he smirked.

Russel gently placed a hand onto Mr. Northern's shoulder.

"Thank you, dear Sir,", he said and shook his hand. "I'm sure you're eager to get things moving", he smiled, as Mr. Northern quickly headed out the door.

"Here we go folks, let's get this show started!", boomed Russel.

Jessie jolted, unsure what he meant.

"What – why are you shouting and where's my surgeon gone?".

"Oh dear, she seems a little muddled everyone", he laughed.

"What the hell are you on about. Who are you talking to and what's so funny?".

"Awww, poor Jessie's scared everyone, isn't that a shame!", he laughed sarcastically.

"I'm not scared! I want to know what's going on! Get Mr. Northern back here right now!".

"I'm afraid he's busy now, so you're stuck with me!".

"I want you to leave, right now! Nurse! Nurse!", shouted Jessie, trying to find the alarm buzzer, but the walls were bare.

"Get my surgeon back you idiot, something went wrong with my operation!".

"Calm down, I'd just like you to watch a few things for a moment. It's the reality T.V. show, Justice, do you remember, the one you were so desperate to watch?", asked Russel.

"Yes, of course I remember, and I don't want to watch it *now* for fuck's sake, get me some help!".

Jessie was instantly silenced, as a mist began to clear, and images started to appear directly in her mind.

"What's going on, what's happening!".

"Just watch the program, relax. We all know how much you enjoyed your visits to the Vault, so you should love this!", sneered Russel.

Jessie tried to deflect the images in her mind, but they were clear, like a vision inside her head.

"It's Sutton. Why are you showing me this now, I don't understand?", she said, as she watched Sutton sitting in a bed, the surroundings hazy and unclear.

"Just pay attention", said Russel.

Jessie watched, as Sutton applied a liquid to each of his fingernails, which was obviously acid, as his fingers began to melt away, disintegrating his flesh to the bone.

She continued to watch, as he took a large brush and applied a brown powder to his face, which had the same effect, eating into his flesh; his cheeks charred, bloody, gaping holes and his skin burnt and hanging from his jaw.

He continued, and applied a green powder onto his eyelids, which instantly turned blood red, as it fizzed and bubbled, eating into his flesh and eyes, leaving him a horrific, grotesque mess – but he didn't even flinch.

"I'm not shocked, it doesn't bother me in the slightest, he deserves everything he gets!", snapped Jessie.

"Well, there you go folks, from its own mouth. I'm glad you agree, as your fate was sealed the second you cast your vote!", said Russel.

"What the fuck are you talking about? Stop this now, I am warning you!", she snarled, her blood now boiling.

"Let's watch a couple more, see if you can work it out", he said.

Once again, Jessie watched Sutton, as he picked up a large heat gun and turned it on.

He aimed it at his head, waving it to-and-fro, not flinching, as his hair curled and singed, the skin on his scalp instantly bubbled and blistered, and his flesh melted away, as blood streamed down his face.

"Has the penny dropped yet?", laughed Russel.

"I still don't understand. Just take me back to the bay, I want to see Nurse Andrews and the girls!".

"Oh yes, of course, your best mates! Well, let's bring them in shall we, come on ladies, in you come!", waved Russel.

A few moments later the three women entered the room.

"Holly, Anna this guy is…", Jessie stopped instantly, and stared at the girls.

"What's going on. You both look so… so different. What's happened to your faces? Nurse Andrews, get me out of here, this guy is crazy!", ranted Jessie, but the three women just stood and stared, then began to laugh, and turned away.

Anna stopped and turned back.

"I'm sorry *Jess*, but you're on your own, enjoy the ride!", she laughed with a wave.

"Wait, wait!", growled Jessie, but the women just looked back, as they held hands and disappeared out the doors.

"You fuckin' bitches! Don't you ever turn your backs on me, get back here! Just you wait, I'll make you all suffer, I swear it! I will slice out your fuckin' tongues!", raged Jessie.

"Ah, here we go, that's more like it. Come on guys, it's time for the vocals!", shouted Russel, throwing his hands in the air.

"You fuckin' prick! If I could get out of this bed I W O…..-U-L-D…..", Jessie's voice suddenly changed to deep, hoarse tones.

"What the hell!", she bellowed.

Jessie froze.

The voice she heard was that of a man, not her own, but she recognised it instantly, it was the voice of Garth Sutton; she had heard it endless times in the Vault!

"Now we're getting somewhere! I think it's time to get her familiar with her surroundings, take it away boys!".

Jessie was suddenly travelling through the misty tunnel, as she had done so many times before. She could hear applause in the distance, as she began to focus.

Her eyes squinted, as a blinding light shone in her face.

Jessie realised that she couldn't move and began to struggle. She tried to sit up but was restrained around her neck and body.

She frantically thrashed around and tried to free herself.

She looked ahead and realised she was in some sort of theatre and was naked, in front of thousands of people. She let out a loud, deep cry.

She shook uncontrollably, as she stared out into the baying crowd.

"Let's introduce you to a few people and give you a rundown of what's been going on", continued Russel.

"Do something! I've lost my mind!", she bellowed, pleading to Mr. Northern, who was sitting in the front row directly ahead of her. He laughed and placed his arm around a woman sitting next to him, and gently kissed her on the side of the head.

Anna, Holly, and Nurse Andrews were in adjacent seats, along with many other people Jessie didn't recognise.

"Let me explain, as I can see you're struggling to take this all in!", said Russel.

The lights dimmed, as Jessie trembled, her eyes desperately darting, no longer able to see into the silenced crowd.

She was back in her room, in her bed.

"Who are you?", asked Russel.

"Oh, thank God!", wailed Jessie, in the voice which she recognised as her own.

"Help me! Something's gone wrong with my surgery, I've lost my mind!", she yelled hysterically.

"Calm down! Who are you, answer the question!", he snapped.

"I'm....I'm Jessie".

"And do you know where you are?".

She was in shock – her eyes frantically searched the room.

"I'm.... I'm at Shorelands", she answered unsurely.

"No. You've never been at Shorelands".

Jessie could hear Russel's voice, but everything was dark.

"You've been held at The People's Justice Organisation. Everything you've experienced, for what you believe has been 8 months, has been controlled by them. They have total control of your mind", said Russel.

"No! This is paranoia! It's all in my head!", shouted Jessie.

"No. *They* are in your head! Occasionally the people you've met have been real, interacting with you directly or through virtual reality, artificial intelligence, and holography. Anna and Holly are the two heroic women who escaped from you. Mr. Northern is the brave father of little Rose Foster and Nurse Andrews, the courageous sister of young Alfie Docherty.

During your preparation to receive the final Justice, they insisted on playing their parts, which has never been attempted before, and even though there were a few glitches, with you jumping to different time frames, it must be said it ran like a dream and they all handled it amazingly! Even I was convinced Richard Foster, playing the part of your surgeon, knew what he was talking about. Abbie and Heather, playing their parts as Anna and Holly, well, I've never witnessed bravery like it, they were incredible.

Anyway, let's get back to you.

You're not Jessie.

Jessie was one of your poor victims. A beautiful, bright, young woman, with her whole life ahead of her. She suffered a terrifying, agonising death in the back of a refuse truck, where you heartlessly bound and dumped her!'".

"This is just in my mind, it's not real. My operation has failed, it will be okay, stay calm, it's not real, it's not real!", ranted Jessie.

"The only things we changed were the way you see yourself, and we took from you your memories and ability to feel pain. We altered nothing of the person you truly are, the character of yourself, inside, your personality and traits, the real you, yet the evilness within you still surfaced. Your brain had been programmed to suppress your memories, but they were free to return at any time, given the correct triggers.

If you had once felt any pity, compassion, or horror at what you were watching, your memory would have returned, but you enjoyed seeing innocent people suffer, and felt nothing but pleasure and arousal. Feelings of enjoyment, excitement, and the hunger for more were all that surfaced.

Let's watch a little more of Justice, the reality program".

"I'm warning you, stop this right now!", growled Jessie, but Russel continued.

"Each and every thought that went through your mind, which like us all, you believe is inside your head, has been loud and clear for us all to hear. Just watch", said Russel.

Again, Jessie could see Sutton sitting in a bed. Nurse Andrews was walking across the room towards a linen cupboard.

"Stuck-up, teasing-bitch. I'd show you what I'm made of if I could get out of this bed! I'd rip those pretty-green-eyes out of your fuckin' head, you're a filthy, fuckin' whore!".

Jessie could clearly hear the thoughts, and the terrifying realisation hit her!

She knew, at that moment, who she *really* was!

She knew they were, in fact, thoughts of her own!

This was real!

She couldn't think, as she was plunged into darkness – the deafening cheers and applause from the crowd echoed in his ears.

"Boys, leave on the thought transmission for now, let's hear what's going on in this sick piece of shits head before we wake up all those pain receptors!".

"Garth Sutton,

welcome to the Final Justice!",

boomed Russel.

22

"Wow, Sutton had no idea, did he Jackie. Have your VIV ready, the finale is up next", laughed Joe, as they sat together on his sofa.

"I'll watch as much as I can, but if I mute the screams don't complain! Thanks for inviting me round, I didn't want to watch this on my own", she smiled.

"I'm really glad you're here", said Joe, as he put his arm around her and pulled her closer.

"Did you watch any of Sutton's memory files?", he asked.

"I watched the horrific murder of his mother and little Bella, and I voted after that. I knew the other files would be too upsetting to watch".

"You wouldn't have seen what he did to Abbie and her fiancée Jason then?".

"No, I just couldn't watch that", she shuddered.

"Oh Jackie, that poor lad. He was strapped to a table for months, slowly having flesh cut away from him day after day, but Sutton ensured he kept Jason alive.

Abbie lay next to him, bound onto a stretcher, her head in a metal brace and her eyes wired open. Sutton forced the poor girl to watch the man she loved suffer in writhing agony, as he was slowly hacked away.

Sutton poured acid over the lad's legs; it was horrendous. It ate through the flesh and bone and even through the table, it was horrific, it really was! Sutton told Abbie to have a good look, as she would be facing the same fate.

Then poor Heather. She was forced to take acid showers. Sutton would even take breaks if she passed out with the agony!

He is pure evil, totally sick and twisted. He's beyond help, that was clear from the start. That demon deserves every second of his sentence… and little Rose…"

"No, stop! Please, I don't want to hear any more. It's enough knowing what he will be feeling is their pain", pleaded Jackie.

"Okay, I'm sorry", apologised Joe.

"Abbie and Heather were especially brave", praised Jackie.

"Yes, they were amazing!

Oh, quick, grab your VIV, it's back on", said Joe excitedly.

The People's Justice Arena

"Welcome back folks! Now it's the moment we've all been waiting for, it's time to turn this evil son of a bitch on!", bellowed Russel.

The atmosphere was electric, with every person standing, as thunderous applause echoed around the arena.

Sutton continued to frantically struggle against the tight straps restraining him.

His memories were now restored, and he knew the terrifying fate which awaited.

He continued to beg and plead for mercy.

"Guys, cut off his vocals for a few moments, this is the families and the victim's time, not his!", instructed Russel.

Sutton was desperately mouthing his words, but no sound could be heard.

Russel invited the victims and their families onto the stage.

"Have you decided who will have the honour of turning on the pain. I know it's a difficult decision, as each of you deserves the pleasure", he asked.

"Yes. We're all in agreement", said Jane Docherty (Nurse Andrews) as she took the hand of Abbie Willis (Anna), who took the hand of Heather Marlow (Holly) until a chain of the victims and their families was formed in front of Sutton.

Richard Foster held his wife in a tight embrace.

Rose's parents looked into each other's eyes, tears streamed down their faces, as they took the lever.

"Sleep easy our beautiful angel!", shouted Richard, as the countdown began.

5…

4…

3…

2…

1!

Lynn and Richard pulled down hard on the handle.

"Now boys, let's hear it!", bellowed Russel, as Sutton's vocals and pain receptors were instantly restored.

Sutton began to experience the beyond evil suffering he had unmercifully inflicted upon each of his victims.

He was hit with the unbearable, agonising affliction, as the nerve endings within his body were restored.

He could feel the excruciating pain of the injuries he had unwittingly inflicted upon himself – the same pain poor Abbie and Heather had suffered, and the immense pain of his severed leg, amputated below the knee.

The families could no longer contain their emotions, as they all hugged, and their tears flowed freely.

Sutton's chilling screams echoed, still heard over the thunderous applause.

***

Jackie suddenly pulled off her visor and threw it onto the floor.

"Oh my God, I can't watch anymore", she cried.

Joe also removed his VIV.

"Really, already?", he asked with surprise.

"Yes, it's just too awful. I know he deserves it, and it's not him I feel for, it's the fact that the pain he's experiencing is that of his poor victims, it's what they endured, it's just too upsetting", she said, wiping away tears.

Joe kissed the back of her hand.

"It's ok Jackie, I know exactly what you mean.

The families never view the memories of the killer, it's strictly forbidden, and most of them leave as soon as the sentence begins.

I can't even begin to imagine how hard it must be for them.

On the one hand, you want to see their killer suffer, but on the other, you know where that suffering came from. Justice is a difficult punishment to handle.

Personally, I would agree to it, as my loved one would be at rest, and I would want their killer to suffer and feel their pain.

The votes will be flooding in now. Once the live show's over, Sutton will be taken to the Justice Organisation, where they'll remove his brain and spinal cord, and it will be sent to the Justice Vault.

There it will be linked to a state-of-the-art artificial body.

They've devised a way to replicate the pain from nociceptors, which I believe are sensory receptors. They can simulate the same pain their victim's experienced through the dummy-body to their brain. Don't ask me all the ins-and-outs of it, I have no idea how it all works, I'm no boffin", laughed Joe. "All I know is, once they're all wired-up, they will feel the pain, along with all the other evil brains in jars", he laughed.

"Good!", said Jackie.

"It's not a nice sight to tell you the truth, in the Justice Vault. There are rows upon rows of brains with their spinal cords hanging inside metal containers, it's quite stomach-turning to see it. The brains will be kept active until their sentence reaches an end, or they become brain dead.

If you have faith, you can take comfort in the belief that they will spend the rest of eternity in Hell", said Joe.

"I don't think I'll visit that vault!", shuddered Jackie.

"No, I wouldn't recommend it either", he said, squeezing her hand.

"Have you heard the latest rumour at the Organisation about their next venture?", asked Jackie.

"Oh, yes, I've heard about it, The Compassion Vault", said Joe.

"Yes, that's it! I've heard that the PJO want to help people understand the pain and suffering of others, in a bid to bring about a more understanding, sympathetic world".

"Well, we work in the right place to see what develops next!", grinned Joe.

23

Serenity Pines
Psychiatric Hospital

"Hello, I'm Mr. Northern the ward psychiatrist, do you remember me, we've spoken several times before?".

"Yes, I remember".

"You seem to have made good progress over the last 8 months Kelly, since accepting your medication. How do you feel within yourself, are you still experiencing strange thoughts?".

(Just tell him what you think he wants to hear, or you're never getting out of here!).

"No, nothing like that. Everything seems to have settled in my mind".

"So, you no longer believe that you're an evil person, that you deserve to be punished?".

"No".

"Do you still feel that people can hear your thoughts, or that you're being watched?".

"Not anymore. I'm feeling much better".

"These are all good signs. After your last assessment, things have improved significantly, the medication has had time to get to work.

Your home-leave also went well. You're no longer displaying signs of acute paranoia, so it's time you were discharged".

(Now, don't go and mess it up, think before you answer!).

"That would be wonderful, I know I'm ready".

"I'll have your release papers and medication prepared, which should be ready for you by the end of the day".

"I'm so much better now".

"Well, feel free to go and pack. Nurse Andrews will inform you when your papers are ready for signature".

"Thank you, Mr. Northern".

"It's good to see you looking and feeling so much better Kelly".

24

Kelly settled in front of her laptop, the email composed and ready to be sent.

She pressed several more layers of electrical tape over the webcam – the lens already obscured by a huge, sticky mound.

Her hand shook violently, as she paused and hovered over the enter key.

'ESCAPE, ESCAPE, ESCAPE', she thumped in a frenzy.

The vision of her thoughts, conceived in the darkest corners of her mind about to become a reality, thrust her into a surge of panic.

Another layer of tape added.

She took a final, lingering drag on her cigarette, before flicking it into the reeking ashtray, brimming with ash and stubs. The embers glowed – still smouldering as she lit another.

She glanced at an old photograph in a wooden frame.

The wall, once a fresh, crisp white, was now a dark mustard.

Years of her life could be counted in the layers of sticky, yellow residue that adhered to the surface – coated in dead fruit-flies and dust.

Behind polished glass, a small child, roughly 6-years-old, stood alone in an overgrown lawn of dandelions.

It was one of the scarce, tangible memories Kelly possessed of herself.

The little girl's honey-brown hair was flicked with strands of caramel, hacked into a short, uneven bob.

Her beige corduroy dungarees bore no design, but for the dirt and grass scuffs decorating the knees – the excess length swallowed her shoes and creased amidst long blades of grass.

A huge, gappy-grin stretched over her small face, with cheeks, so red, they appeared almost chafed. Her wide, hazel eyes glistened, radiating a bright spark of hope.

"Poor naive kid", whispered Kelly.

She saw little resemblance to her older self.

Her hazel eyes were now dulled, carrying the weight of anxiety and fear beneath them.

The brown-golden-crown was now a flat umber – the flecks of sunlight replaced with brittle, grey strands.

Years of smoking had receded her gums, her remaining teeth were now a shade lighter than her hair – a once petite frame now substantial and full.

She grabbed the open vodka bottle beside her, tilting it eagerly, and swigged the last drops, shaking the bottle violently over her open mouth, in desperation, for any remaining dregs.

The smooth glass suddenly slipped between her sweaty, yellow fingers, and bounced, as if in slow-motion, across the keyboard.

Message Sent flashed on the screen.

She leapt from her seat in a drunken stupor, desperately scrambling for the mouse.

   "Undo. Undo. Oh my God, undo!", she screamed from the pit of her lungs.

It was too late.

Message Delivered.

25

"Congratulations, you have a healthy baby girl!", beamed the midwife, as she lay the newborn onto her mother's chest.

"Have you agreed on a name yet?", she asked.

"Ivy, we've decided on calling her Ivy", said the mother, and looked to her partner, who nodded in approval.

"That's beautiful, I love that name", smiled the midwife. "If you could read the Global Anti-Virus Vaccine leaflet and sign the permission slip on the back, I'll prepare Ivy's dose – should you decide to go ahead. As I'm sure you're aware, the New World Law mandates that anyone wishing to receive medical care, whether free or private, must have received the GAVV vaccination. While this is not compulsory, admission to medical establishments will be denied if declined. The policy applies to private practices, general practitioners, hospitals, dentists, and more – please refer to the accompanying booklet for a full list of services affected.

Additionally, any child who has not been protected by the GAVV will not be entitled to state education or childcare".

"Yes, of course, please go ahead, we want Ivy to be protected", said the mother, and she and her partner signed the form.

"Here we go little lady, a small scratch and then it's bath time.

Tomorrow, all being well with your brave mummy, you should be allowed home", smiled the midwife.

ORWELL DEPARTMENT
Mind/Visual Surveillance

NAME: Ivy Louise Wilson

GLOBAL VACCINATION NO:
122028/86972463

NANOBUG IMPLANTED:
20-12-2084 (dob)

VISUAL RECORDING STATUS:
Active

THOUGHT PROCESSOR:
Active

RECORDING FROM:
20:58, 20:59, 21:00, 21:01, 21:02,
21:03.......

26

Serenity Pines
Psychiatric Hospital

I stared at that key for hours – my hand trembled as it hovered, and withdrew, time and again. I snatched to 'undo', but it was too late, it was done. Gone. I knew I had sealed my own fate. I should never have put it into words. They told me it was paranoia. There's nowhere to run anymore, nowhere to hide. They're after me now, I'm certain of it. I'm finished. Am I crazy? I must be crazy! It's just a story. Fiction. No, they're wrong! They believe they hold the answers to reality, but how could they know? How could anyone *really know*? It's all in your mind! It's what I was taught – we were taught. That's all that I am – we are. Information, stored, filed. Memories. We are but a matter of grey. As I wrote that book, I knew it couldn't be me writing that story. It was planted for me to find. A library of words buried, living in that place, the dark, shameful place. But I kept pushing, hunting, searching for the truth. I've delved deep. Those fleeting, shameful thoughts, those which I would fervently deny, they claw endlessly to the forefront of my mind.

They haunt me. Disgust me. What if *they* really *do* know what I'm thinking? The shame would break me. Is it only me? Could it be the same for us all? Are they listening to you too? Are they watching you too? Big Brother is Watching You! That smart television with its watchful, hidden eye, tracking, listening, recording. Each webcam scanning your life, each keypress stamped in your file. Every shameful, fleeting moment etched in stone. I really must sleep – but what if we awake, strapped to that stretcher, our eyes blinded by that light!

'The Light' – a beautiful brightness, a presence described by many as divine; a warm, spiritual, transitional awakening. Death invites us to it. The thought now chills me to the core. That light! I can only hope, even pray, that I am, indeed, mad. My head is splitting in two. My face feels numb. I can't see clearly. The light, it's so blinding…

Please don't let me go into the light.

Please don't let me go into the light.

Please don't let me go…

Chamber Of Victory ID.19

Mail Interception

Status: CRITICAL

Miss. Kelly Arlington
Nanobug: 78890235/f-0405-1970

LEVEL 10
TERMINATION
26-08-2024

Life File Info

Attachment scanned
DOCUMENT - 2084

"She was a troubled soul wasn't she, but still, it's such a shame".

"54-years old, no age to die is it".

"Apparently, she suffered a brain aneurysm. Dropped dead on the spot, gone!".

"Most of her life was spent in mental health institutions, that's where she was during her final moments, ranting crazy ideas. Sad really".

"She used to say some pretty weird things though. Covid vaccinations laced with some sort of recording, mind reading device was her latest conspiracy theory. She was quite mad I would say!".

"Yes, that's true, she most certainly was!".

"Well, even so, may she rest easy in the *Eternal Light*".

The End

For my boys

Connor & Cameron

<u>In Loving Memory</u>

Mum

Gill

Mr. Paul Sharpling

Printed in Great Britain
by Amazon

56779343R00099